S0-APY-967

Cold Eye

To my niece, Stacy Pendergrast

and

my granddaughter,

Lauren Skinner Lomax

CONTENTS

Cold Eye

1.

My frog voice set the low decibel standard on radio station WKLR. "Keep a cool tool, an open mind and roll out easy ... "It's Monday morning with Furious."

Out of bed before dawn for the graveyard shift, I tripped over the obstacle course of her shoes, stumbling across the cold floor to the bathroom and switched on the light for the morning ritual: scrubbing teeth, gargling and taming my wiry red hair. Again I dodged her shoes--spiked heels, tennis shoes, leopard slip-ons, hiking boots, gathering my jeans and shirt from the bedpost, my flip-flops from under the bed.

The lump of Jody shifted and turned under the gray blanket, groaning in her sleep-matted voice, the same sort of bluesy sound I'd be playing at the station in half an hour. I'd been home from Ireland for three days and we'd yet to have sex.

I hoped she was groaning for me.

She was a week late on her monthly breast exam, something we always did together. Gently I turned her over. I have always been a boob man; hers small, yet perfect. She seemed easy with it at first, her big brown eyes shining up at me, and I was figuring on a score. Nonetheless, I was thorough with the exam, fingers marching over each inch of both boobs, which unnerved her. She pushed me back and began to knead my chest, circling my nipples and digging in with her long fingernails before stopping abruptly. Her index finger marked a spot and wheedled it.

"Check this out," she said, her frown a serious crevice between her brows. She began stroking the spot, at the same time guiding my fingers to the tiny kernel buried in my nipple.

"A zit," I said, dismissing it.

Magic broken, I rolled out of bed again, my fingers sliding across the chest of drawers, hunting for the key ring.

"Go back to Ireland," she said, rolling onto her side.

Blues: just *the way it is* at 5 a.m. on a cold autumn morning. I jingled the keys in her ear, patted her on the butt and headed for the door. She'd threatened to leave me at least once a month for the three years we'd lived together. I chalked it off as part of her routine.

"The cult awaits me. Turn up your radio!"

"Turn out the light."

2.

During the pledge drive—"for all you deadbeat listeners out there, cough it up for all volunteer WKLR"—the glut of emails and letters addressed to *Fury's Blues* proved I counted for something in the world, connecting to the fans, if not always to Jody.

At the WKLR celebration—the goal of sixty-five thousand had been reached, and the volunteers were ecstatic--station manager Mitch Mancini's rare smile was so wide it showed all his crooked teeth. In a joy-killing tone Jody whispered, "File down those incisors, he might look close to normal."

I passed on Mitch's condition without comment, yet there was something mordant about teeth, probably the reason dentists commit suicide more often than other professionals. At least Mitch hadn't overheard her. " Celebrate radio," I said to remind her why we'd come to the party in the first place. The station was fiscally sound, at least for another season.

In that little black dress she loved wearing, Jody held the wine glass aloft, her straight blonde hair framing the face of perpetual disdain.

Just as Mitch came up to greet us, she said "Why radio when you've got IPOD? You people were pulled into the 21st Century by a choke chain."

Mitch assumed his manager's voice. "Jody, when people turn on the radio, they're listening to the same music *at the same time.* Call it a spiritual connection."

"Hear it live at the High Tone." Her lips were red with wine. She took another sip.

"Radio beams into hundreds of houses," continued Mitch, wind-milling his hands and spreading his arms. "Like the sun and the moon, if you know what I mean."

"Guglielmo Marconi!" I said loudly in a voice full of scorn. Like Jody, I'd had way too much wine and couldn't stop myself. "A man more important than Christopher Columbus or Amerigo Vespucci or even Magellan! A man who explored the world of sound for God's sakes!"

"Now, now, Franko," said Mitch. "Turn down your volume. Marconi wasn't altogether a forward thinking scientist. He viewed x-ray as invasion of privacy––thought you could see through clothing and view a person's private parts."

"Okay, but I actually stood in the bog on the west coast of Ireland where Marconi set up his first trans-mitter! Jody just has no appreciation, no sense of reverence. Marconi is Patron Saint of Radio!"

"Franko, you are *so* Catholic."

In Jody's cold eyes I saw a further decline of our relationship––the beginning of the end. Marconi *was* founder and soul of my universe, yet I hadn't meant to canonize him. In the flurry of my own words, I'd gone over the top, done myself in. Nothing new there.

"Marconi was no saint," said Mitch. "In fact he was quite the womanizer."

"A sinner," corrected Jody. "I knew there was something to like."

3.

Prior to the diagnosis, as if by some premonition, I laid in a supply of hats, most of them bought in Ireland. Call me Bartholomew O'Cubbins.

The yen for the hats came after I visited Trinity College and the Book of Kells. In a room packed with reverent visitors so silent as to be startling, I was struck by the beauty of the monks' transcription of the New Testament on parchment made from calf hide after first scraping and then rubbing it with either lime or excrement. I rubbed my own hands together as if I, too, might have something to contribute: sloughed skin or spit.

Still in a reverie over the exacting, exquisite work, I climbed the stairs to the library and into the Long Room where many of the oldest and most important books held by the college are displayed--Joyce's *Ulysses* along with works by W.B. Yeats and illustrations by his brother, the artist Jack Yeats. Busts of philosophers and writers set on pedestals filled the center aisle. I spent time with Jonathan Swift. Life today, how might Swift satirize it? Every day thousands of babies die in Africa, so many you couldn't eat them as Swift might have suggested.

I spent time with a fifteenth century harp, emblem of early bardic society. I wanted to pluck it. Instead I took in deep breaths of the mustiness, filling myself with the floating dust. Later, when I recalled the experience to Jody, she asked if the room was climate controlled. She missed the point.

Out on the street again, wanting to hold the reverie in my head, I stopped in at a haberdashery to purchase a tweed woolen cap. I was easy with the drizzle as I walked through St. Stephen's Green and up to the Liffey—O'Connell Street, Parnell Square, Mary's Lane. Bachelor's Walk was my personal labyrinth. In fact I felt right at home in "Dear dirty, Dublin" midst the bustle of its people—some of them reddish-blond and blue-eyed with red splotchy faces as familiar to me as my own face in the mirror. In the days that followed I bought several more hats.

4.

The night I came home to Memphis, I entered my house and set down my suitcase. Jody walked. Into the living room holding Little Ben in her arms. He yowled and wrested free of her, then shot to the pantry and disappeared behind the cans of soup and the cat food.

"It's going to be a long night," I said.

"This morning I had him dipped. He's still upset with me."

Unlike his progenitor, the late Big Ben — *B Nips*, his nickname, carved on the stone marker out back over the burial site––Little Ben is antisocial, a trait he shares with Jody.

"It's a trade off between you two," I said. "You won't talk to *him* ... he won't bite *you*."

"So you got your fill of the old sod?"

"I could live there, actually."

"What's to stop you?"

I poked a yardstick in the corners of the pantry to stir Little Ben.

"There," said Jody. "Behind the V-8."

Little Ben's tail poked out as a tease. I grabbed hold and gave it a yank. He hissed and darted out of the kitchen. "Not much of a homecoming," I said, and popped a Killian's to soothe my hurt feelings and turned my attention to Jody.

"Miss Doolin," I said in my formal voice. "Would you like to know about the village of Doolin? I walked across many kilometers of countryside from Lahinch toward the Cliffs of Moor, but before I went up the road to see the full spectacle of the cliffs, I turned the opposite way, down to Doolin."

Swift was all over her face now. "I hope you didn't go out of your way for me. Doolin is a surname, not a choice."

She did not want to hear anymore about it, but the floodgates were open. "Doolin is a tidy little fishing village. From there you catch the ferry for the Aran Isles."

She listened with bored patience as I extolled over *Inis Mean* and its *Leaba Dhiramuid is Grainne*––a collapsed Neolithic wedge tomb named after the tragic lovers from Irish mythology; and *Inis Mor's Clochan na Carraige*––the only perfect stone dwelling on the Aran Islands.

I recalled the high cliffs for her, the rugged landscapes and the ancient fort, all relics of Gaelic Civilization and of Irish, which after centuries of British rule and suppression of the native tongue, is once again the official language of the people. For a moment I imagined all of her cylinders secretly firing at me from behind the blank expression, then back to the Aran Isles I travelled, yammering each detail of my journey as her big dark eyes rolled up in the top of her head and yes, I was merely talking to myself. I'd lost her somewhere between *Inis Meain* and *Inis Mor*. Intrepidly I boarded the ferry again, heading back to Doolin, holding my guts—rough sea but no regrets, no more than I regretted Jody Doolin or the cats.

She stood in Tree, her number one favorite yoga position. Jody numbers only her favorites: Little Ben number one cat; avocado, number one food; Bogle's Petite Syrah number one wine. Once upon a short time ago I'd been her number one man. Finding her balance, she spread her branches, her light brown hair a nice place for a nesting bird. I halfway expected Little Ben to climb her.

It came to me then that fall was the only time we'd been of the same mind—Jody and me—together, breathing as we did, the fatalism blowing through that season. Why hadn't I told her about the diagnosis of my breast cancer sooner? In not doing so, I'd denied her the satisfaction of having been the discoverer, my personal Columbus or Magellan. If I said it now, after the passage of so long a time, she'd turn Swiftian on me. *That* I would regret.

5.

For all of you who have trouble following me, park your shoes and put on your cross trainers. One step forward; two or three steps back; run in place; jump side-to-side. Avoid potholes and speed bumps.

When I told my sister Geraldine I would undergo

day surgery to remove the lump from my hairy breast, she was stunned to disbelief.

"It should be me," she said in a spit of jealousy, sibling rivalry to the end.

Geraldine saw herself as the tragic heroine.

"Angel of Death passed you by," I said. "You've been slighted."

"Not funny," she said. "Take it back."

I'd said the wrong thing, a habit leftover from our childhood, and immediately regretted it. "Don't start biting your nails again."

Geraldine poked me in the ribs, under the circumstance her elbows damn vicious. She said, "THUMB is still available. Civil Liberties hasn't got wind of it yet."

I agreed to let her drive me to the surgery center, but first she had to promise three things: she would make an appointment for a mammogram; she'd tell no one about my cancer; and she'd wear a proper chauffeur's cap. Then I changed the subject to the demands of her career as a flipper. "If the surgery is a success, I'll invest in your flipping business."

"I still don't understand why you quit your job. Flipping isn't steady. You'll need steady money to pay your insurance premiums. They don't call it Cobra for nothing."

Geraldine did not believe in quitting anything.

The little dig hurt my feelings. I could see my insurance slithering away from me. Yet I'd been working for years at Artique and had both a rainy day account and what I perceived as adequate investments. Behind my sealed lips I sucked on each incisor--the phrase *long in the tooth* came into my head. My predicament was Goddamn ridiculous. Dammit to hell, I was a man. A forty-eight year old man.

6.

In Sligo I stayed overnight at a B&B run by a nice old English couple. The woman brought tea and square lemon cakes into the parlor anchored by Victorian artifacts, possibly inherited from ancestors who'd served in Egypt or Burma. Her husband brought me a day old newspaper, neatly folded. Though retired from an insurance agency, he wore a tie in his own home.

She wore a dark floral dress appropriate for church and a hair net to keep her dark coiffure neatly in place. She claimed to spend one afternoon per week at the beauty parlor getting her hair washed and set. It seemed a matter of pride.

Slicked down with pomade, his hair was his wife's same color—way too dark for their aged skin tones, and I felt certain they'd done it to each other.

They left me in the silence of the room accented

by their daughter's bridal portrait and the dried bouquet, prominent in the center of the mantle. Aside the fireplace, on a shelf heavy with an old set of encyclopedias, was a small photo of the daughter with her American husband and their two children living in Milwaukee, and below it a shelf devoted to a pair of bronzed baby shoes and a photo of the daughter blowing out two candles on her birthday cake. Above me on the second floor, the footsteps of the old couple failed to muffle the stalking noise--a certain presence in the house of which they seemed unaware.

The next morning, after a sleepless night in a tiny windowless room kin to a tomb, I put on the heavy sweater that both Mitch and Jody had insisted I pack--and left the house earlier than planned. In the rain, I visited the ruins of Sligo Abbey and walked by the Yeats' Room in the Sligo County Museum and Library. I returned to the house to pick up my one piece of luggage in the entryway as prearranged and hung the door key on the key holder the woman had shown me. They were gone, the house solid in silence, and I found myself whispering "Goodbye" for what reason I've yet to figure.

In spite of the heavy sweater, I shivered as I wheeled my bag through the misty streets and caught the bus to Drumcliff, settling myself in a window seat.

If Jody had a change of heart and married me, would we become more alike? Would we, in later years, dye each other's hair?

The bus rumbled past thatched cottages and sheep nibbling grass, a countryside that looked as I'd expected, but was soon startled by the effects of emigration brought on by the growing computer industry—garish modern housing and busy road construction in opposition to the otherwise pastoral setting. I hoped my ability to forget what I chose not to remember would sustain me.

Near the foothill of Ben Bulben, I stepped from the bus into the cold wind and rain. On the property of Yeats' burial site, fenced in stacked stone, I found shelter in a little shop for visitors. I fueled on rich potato soup, crusty bread and hot tea.

Outside under the watchful eyes of a murder of crows vying for nests in the trees around the churchyard, I visited St. Columba's Church where Yeats' grandfather had preached. Outside again I stood at Yeats' grave and read his epitaph:

Cast a cold Eye

On life, on death.

Horseman, pass by

Behind a cloud the sun was low in the sky. I walked across the road and around the old silo that seemed at once *lifted from* and *held to* the ground on which it rested. I then recognized the presence of despair. As I walked across the road and stood before a ruined cottage, waiting for the bus, I raised my shoulders and did not breathe. I would head west toward the site of Marconi's first transatlantic transmitter station, into the setting sun. It's the journey that counts.

Near Clifden I hiked along the remote coastline and came upon what remains of the station—wrecked in 1922 by Irish irregulars as part of their struggle for Home Rule—and stood in the bog surveying the ruins left as a monument to Marconi's great pioneering effort.

Later, what lingered in my mind--even more than the ruins—was the story told to me at the end of the day by a villager at the local pub at Clifden about a beached whale's distress and how it had captured the whole village's sense of urgency. Every able-bodied man, woman and child formed a bucket brigade and for several days worked tirelessly to save the whale. In spite of the effort, the whale died. The mourning began. The scientist who came to investigate the death and to determine the whale's age, failed in his assignment.

7.

Before my trip to Ireland, I gave Mitch the dates

of my journey. He was less than happy. "I still say a whole month is too long. Listen to your fans," he'd said, handing me a letter:

Dear Furious,

You've got the spin, man. Will miss the Monday morning dirge. What's in Ireland, man? Give it up for the working folks and come on home soon.

Love reigns, Haybale

"Mitch, I'm fresh out of bald-headed woman songs. I need a break."

"You've got *The Ever-loving Jody Blues*," he said as he reached out to pat my shoulder, an obvious attempt at consolation. I stepped back to avoid his touch. He's a much-loved fag. Coming soon was the annual Southern Confederation of Gay Men's Spring Ball, an exclusive seasonal fantasia months in the planning. Mitch was committee chairman. He fretted over the decorations as well as his own costume, the exact nature of both things tightly held secrets. There was no convincing him to take one lover at a time, his eyes red-rimmed from lack of sleep. Member of the Gay Italian-American Anti Defamation League, he accepted personal criticism as condemnation, so I kept my mouth shut.

"What about earning a living?" he asked. "Can you afford to take so much time off?"

In truth I was sick of my real job as public

relations coordinator of ARTIQUE, a company that sells artifacts procured from unknown sources. I felt complicit, something kin to a grave robber.

"Instead of exploiting someone else's heritage, I want to explore my own."

"Heritage of bad teeth," said Mitch, oblivious of his own dental problems. I did have a slight gap between my two front teeth. "Sign of a liar," Jody insisted. She went on to say — she *always* went on to say something more — I lied only to myself.

A zydeco two-step in the sound room blared from the wall speakers in the reception area where we stood. It was the theme song of *Corky's Cajun Fest*. I tapped my heel to the backbeat. "Corky agreed to sit in for you on Mondays, but only if he can alternate zydeko with blues. Your fans will go nuts." He clasped his hands together and sighed overlong. "Changing the subject, I was wondering if you'd mind taking Mike Finn's favorite wool sweater with you. He dreamed of going to Ireland. It would be something like sending him."

Finn had recently died of aids. "If I have room in the suitcase, I'll take it," I said, wondering if the sweater had been cleaned. Jody had been part of Mitch's brigade that took turns bringing food to Finn.

Mitch placed his hand over his heart and sighed. "My people come from Palermo. Some day I'm going over." He picked up the mail scattered on the floor below the brass mail slot and began sorting it into stacks on his desk. From inside the station the fire engine red letters painted on the storefront window read DLVW. Black and white photos of the musicians lined the newly painted, electric yellow walls, the photographs now moodier by contrast. I rarely travelled and felt the first twinge of separation anxiety. I'd miss the station—my home away from home—and I'd miss the last stages of the renovation so long in the planning.

Across the street at the Green Beetle, Negress May Luna, wearing espadrilles, teetered on a ladder as she unscrewed a light bulb over the door. I touched the place on my chest where Jody first felt the zit days ago. My mother had died of breast cancer. For a moment I went dark. At worst, I told myself, it was the first stage of a slow festering boil.

I left the station and crossed the street to assist the exotic Negress May who sported new reddish-blonde dreadlocks the texture of steel wool.

"Nice hair, May," I said, steadying the ladder.

"Inspiration, Darlin'. That's you."

Her hair color was similar to mine: Negress and me, a couple of clowns. She handed me the spent bulb and screwed a new one into the socket. Descending, she patted my hair. A cloud passed overhead. It lingered over the sun before moving on. I folded my hands across my chest, a sneaky way of hugging myself. What if the pimple wasn't just *that*?

Watching us from the tattoo parlor was Timbo Grice, the tall, pale skinny tattoo artist propped against his open doorway smoking a cigarette, sleeves rolled up 50's style. Skinny black snakes, self-inflicted, ran the length of his long, knotty arms on skin the thickness of leather. When he'd tattooed the butterfly on Jody's fair-skinned shoulder blade, I'd nearly fainted.

"What's new, Timbo?" I called. Timbo held open his shirt and unveiled the exotic bird with exquisite orange and purple plumage, colors as hot as a Memphis summer. "Franko, when you're ready, I'll do you a lizard or a crocogator."

Not for the faint of heart, I was thinking. "When I get back, maybe."

"Mail Call!" hollered Mitch from the door. Overhead a flock of geese traveled the sky as I crossed the street. Mitch handed over a stack of fan mail. "You're not even gone yet and they already miss you." He fanned the envelopes, an automaton of bird wings in sync with the zydeco. There was profundity in what he'd said, the air suddenly stirred by the palpitation of wing beats and fervent squawks. Millions of birds travel over the Mississippi Fly Zone on their way to the nesting grounds in the marshes of Louisiana. To be in league with them, to just fly away, seemed too easy.

8.

In the west of Ireland a gray horse eating grass in a field took a break to scratch his face with his hind hoof. People on the bus laughed and applauded. A major itch, a major scratch.

Late afternoon, as the bus rolled on, the bus driver switched on Galway Bay Radio. Mary Kate Sullivan announced the names and biographical data of the recently departed and gave the funeral arrangements: Padriac Francis O'Flynn of Oughterard succumbed to an aneurysm, Wednesday's funeral mass 10 o'clock at St. Moira's Church. Mary Margaret Larkin of Recess went with cancer, her funeral mass at St. Mary's 10 o'clock on Thursday. Michael Christopher Wade was run over by a tour bus from Dublin, his graveside service at the Liscanor Cemetery, 10 o'clock Wednesday. "We at Galway Bay Radio offer our prayers and our sympathy to all families."

The broom waved in the light wind as a mournful fiddle brought the radio wake to an end. In somnolent retreat, the sheep lay down in the fields and Mary Kate's voice retired to my head. If voices stayed with us, we'd always have guides.

Now I lay me sheep to sleep
I pray the lord me sheep to keep
If they should die before they sleep
I pray the lord their souls to bleat

9.

At home I told Mitch about the death announcement and immediately he wanted to begin a new WKLR show called Underground, devoted to the newly departed. I was anxious to be distracted from my medical problem and to resume Fury's Blues.

"We've already got alternative and cult."

"Franko, the dead don't get much attention. A few lines in the morning paper. Housewife, widow of the late So & So. Welder for So & So Brothers. Computer programmer for So & So Limited. Chief Cake Baker for So & So Bakery. What does that say about a life?"

"Depends on the cakes," I said, failing to restrain myself. "Look Mitch, a death on Tuesday is old news by Friday."

His dimples were impressive. He postured himself and seemed to grow taller. Clearly he wasn't listening.

"It looks like I have breast cancer," I admitted. "And yes, I've been in denial."

Whatever he thought about a man having breast

cancer wasn't revealed in his face. "I ran into Jody yesterday. She said nothing about your bad luck. Does she even know about this?"

10.

Geraldine drove me to the biopsy and the MRI. She researched my medical predicament and knew more about it than I did. No complaints here about her attention or concern. I made Geraldine tell Jody about the cancer. Jody was upset and refused to speak to me. "She should have heard it from you, Franko."

Over a period of several weeks I had three mammograms as well as a biopsy and the MRI, and prior to surgery, the insertion of pins to guide the surgeon to the calcifications, which are microscopic tumors. For the biopsy and pin insertion, I lay flat on the table with my nipples over two holes, under which the mammography machine relayed the images to the screen on a shelf a few feet away. At one time or another, four radiologists explored my cancerous breast, the pictures of it like a mass in outer space. The radiologists—Doctors Love, Gayden, Armstrong and Glen--were female astronauts dedicated to keeping me earthbound while they, one by one, visited the moon.

My chest didn't offer much in the way of protrusion, forcing Dr. Love to make adjustments, turning me on my side to further poke my chest into the hole. "Sorry we had to shave you again," she said. "You've got what we call a real *patch of thatch*." She was an old doctor with a lovely old face and genteel manner. She studied my position, her brow furrowing in concentration.

"Size A minus," I speculated. "Sorry to put you out."

"No apology necessary. It's not often we get to torture a man."

I admit I enjoyed being rare. Still, the shaved breast didn't seem to belong to me, a man unlucky enough to find himself in this predicament. Consider me the boob.

On the screen the area in question was a glowing white orbit, a celestial body with dark tracks, traces and lagoons. As a boy I'd learned that stars are dead, at the time an almost morbid disclosure, but now the idea of shimmering in the sky was stellar, of certain ambition, and I imagined myself up there beaming light in the great galaxy as a beacon upon which others, seamen for instance, could rely. A shame the other one couldn't participate in the uplifting experience, its ambiance.

Years back, when Hail Bop appeared in the sky, I drove to the river many times over to witness it, as if a recurring miracle. In its glow there was solemnity and I thought of it as a formal prayer, the expression of which I could actually see, and I wished it would stay on forever.

One evening at home, as I stepped out on the stoop and prized the cap from a bottle of Killian's Red and kicked it into the flower bed--for all us boobs, beer caps make a nice ground cover--I looked up and saw Hail Bop above a tree snapped by the ice storm a few years before. The branches of taller trees formed a canopy above it, a circle as it was, so that Hail Bop appeared to be centered in a wreath. Why I had not noticed it before confirmed what Jody had said. "When it comes to recognizing something staring you right in the face, you might as well be blind."

On that same evening, waiting for Jody to come home, I'd left the door unlocked in the usual way, and though she knew the door would be unlocked, as always she rang the bell. As always, my anticipation rose steadily as I listened to her footsteps walking through the living room into the kitchen and out the screen door. A shiver ran my back as she approached me in the dark, still gazing at Hail Bop. Before tilting her face skyward, she looked at me. We held hands in silence.

The euphoria of outer space, the recollection of my connection to it and to Jody, was soon exhausted by pain--the side of my face pressed to the table, my neck as if in a vice.

"Are you all right?" asked Dr. Love.

"Okay," I assured her.

The ratcheting of the suctioning device retrieving pieces of me filled my head. The mammogram screen featured regret ... what was, was no more. I closed my eyes and took slow, deep yoga breaths the way Jody does when she wants to escape something unpleasant. Over and again, four drawn in, four pushed out, I drifted back to a time when breasts were the utmost mystery of my universe.

11.

It began with a telephone call from Grace Vanucci. She'd written me chatty letters when I was away at Camp Joseph of the Ozarks—this from a girl who was just shy of mute—so no surprise she'd be waiting for me when I returned to Memphis.

"Father Stan wants to meet with the Saints at the rectory tonight. See you on the playground later."

As if I'd just won a prize, I hung up the phone with a big smile on my face.

My friends and I were on a prowl that summer, thirteen-year-old punks, our restlessness noted with some disdain by Father Stan. His mission was to snag at least one of us for the priesthood.

Through baseball and our duties as altar boys, he

had us pretty much under control. Don't serve, don't play.

He was less successful with the girls, especially the Seven Saints. He'd cautioned us to keep our distance from them, but the summons by our favorite priest set the Seven Saints apart from other girls and confirmed the way we thought of them--bold, otherworldly.

The aforementioned Grace, along with Ursula Favaza and Lena Lorenzi, had skipped school that spring; earlier in summer Grace and Ursula had attempted to catch a freight train; and just before I'd gone off to camp, Grace, Ursula, Lena, Liza Mahoney and Camille Smyczek had broken into a vacant house.

If ethnic cleansing had been an issue in our old neighborhood, there were plenty of groups to choose from, including the blacks who lived on the fringes. At any rate, the Saints were in a state of flux, united only when it suited them. Out of the seven, only two members, Theresa Kinsella and Theresa Lenzini — one for Avila, the other for Lisieux — met the true definition of Sainthood. The other five Saints merely tolerated Avila and Lisieux, until they had something to confess. It was only a matter of time.

On that sticky summer's night the four of us — Joe Mickey, Phillip Santini, Jimmy Harahan and me were crouched outside the open window of the receiving room of the rectory, eavesdropping on the proceedings. Once the Saints were assembled in the room and seated in a circle around the table under the dim lights and flickering candles, Father Stan asked Grace to lead the Rosary. Smoke drifted from the window.

Heart of our world, the lighting and extinguishing of candles seemed to burn away the seasons. We were caught between the smoke and the monotone of moribund prayers drifting from the rectory and the heat and humidity of summer outside. I envisioned myself as a wax figure, melting before I'd even lived.

The Rosary ended. In his sternest voice, Father Stan set upon the Saints with Thomas a' Kempis. The Saints were in for it and so were we. Time for meeting them on the playground would pass into oblivion. In the passage Father read, Mary Magdalene repented of her sins while bearing testimony of her sorrow.

Leave it to Kempis and Father Stan to keep from us exactly what she'd done, to tease us with details, admitting only that she'd kissed, incessantly, Our Saviour's feet. In reaction we nudged elbows and sputtered laughter. Imagine how it might be if you wore the same pair of tennis shoes in Palestine for months on end, then aired them.

All I could think of was athlete's foot, desert

fleabites and the smell. Father Stan droned on about our debts and about Jesus' patient forbearance and patient love — patience his theme — gradually raising his voice until he had Mary Magdalene not only kissing Jesus' feet, but also weeping on them. Father Stan just didn't get it. If I'd been required to kiss feet--even Grace Vanucci's--I'd have wept buckets too.

Father Stan wasn't subtle. There was no segue from one theme to the next.

"Boys are weak," he announced, then counselled the Saints not to lead us down any alley where the tangle of honeysuckle spilled its erotic perfume. "You have the power to distract them from their higher purpose. Holding hands with girls in tight sweaters and ballet slippers leads young men astray."

Father Stan made no mention of us leading them anywhere, so the next day when Grace Vanucci called to let me know she was alone in the house for the day, I washed my feet, brushed my teeth, combed my hair, and making the Sign of the Cross as I passed Little Flower Church, ran the five blocks to her house, bounded up the steps and across the landing, and stood cloistered in the alcove of her front door. Taking a deep breath, I rang the bell.

The door opened slowly, the way it does in books. I traveled her. Her lips were ripe with several coats of Orange Flip. She wore a pink baby doll blouse and what I remembered as last year's white shorts. Around her waist was a white cinch belt. She was barefoot and busty and it was all for me.

Neither of us said one word. From the living room she led me through the French doors into a small room with a nubby green couch and tropical draperies in a large-scaled print of green foliage and huge yellow bananas, in what seemed an island paradise.

Father Stan was wrong about the ballet slippers. Through steam and low-lying fog I caught sight of her orange toenails.

Grace put a stack of old 45's on the record player, both inherited from her older brother who had died in Korea. A photograph had been turned toward the wall and I thought it was of him. We danced, awkwardly at first, then like two pressed boards, moving an inch at a time. I ignored the ceramic bust of the pious Madonna praying from the shelf.

"Earth Angel," I said and just left it at that.

Grace's family was mafia affiliated, and even though she'd suddenly forgotten how to talk, she was definitely in charge. I succumbed to her without the slightest resistance. Sin, what sin? If she'd wanted me to jump off the Mississippi-Arkansas Bridge, I would have considered it my great privilege. If she'd put out a contract on someone--Mrs. Portugal the dietician at school comes to mind--I would have killed without

36

conscience. Grace had the power to send me straight to hell.

The kisses were sensational, never innocent. Her chest rose and fell against mine. Should I touch her breasts? I made animal noises and tried to suppress them. My head was swimming. my body sweating.

The phone rang loudly — so much so I thought it was the church bell as she slipped out of my arms and into the hall to answer it. Just as quickly she returned to say her Mother was on the way home.

"Go," she said in no uncertain terms.

I felt dazed as she led me through the French doors. Without so much as a goodbye, she pushed me over the threshold, shut the front door with a bang and clicked the lock. I was on the outside, she on the inside.

I was mortally attached to sin now, to the smell of it. I could no more leave the premises than a bee sipping nectar from a rose.

My ear pressed to the front door, I could hear her footsteps travelling toward the back of the house. Slowly, stealthily, I slipped down the shady side of the house through the azalea bed toward the roaring air conditioner, ducking under branches of dogwoods, large old shrubs and trees trembling with bird sounds. From inside I heard the scraping noise of the chair. The air conditioner blew hot air in my face.

I climbed the trunk of the oak tree and spied on her through the window. She sat at a glass-topped table in the breakfast room, pouring Coke over ice and eating potato chips. How could she swallow? Having lived, having felt the earth quake beneath your feet, how could you then accept Extreme Unction?

She'd changed into a short-sleeved white blouse with a little round collar that appeared to me as a fallen halo. If I'd chanced exposure on the sunny side of the house, I might have caught sight of her bare breasts between outfits. Now she unfastened the cinch belt, hung it on the back of the chair and took a deep breath, which in turn sucked all the air out of me. My arms grew tired, my legs wobbling on the branch, and I held tight to keep from falling. If I couldn't see her breasts, at least I get another glimpse of her orange toes.

To steady myself, I reached for a branch just above my head. My feet slipped, my legs treading air and rustling leaves as the branch moaned and creaked.

Suddenly at the window her eyes were big, her orange mouth wide open. She yanked the cord on the blinds, cutting me off, the ground resonating with my fall. Monkey me, monkey havoc, monkey hate. The birds dove and pecked me.

12.

After each chemotherapy session, my brain became scrambled, like an email message in code. I blinked on and off to rid my head of the figures and symbols. Once the brain cleared of static, my memories seemed to glow. The three years Jody and I had lived together came seeping into my mind like floodwater inching up a stoop. I revered the moments spent with her, tension et al.

On Jody's moving day, I wore the do-rag provided me by Negress May who had also brought word of Timbo's offer to tattoo a replacement nipple free of charge, which I was considering as I poked around Jody's wicker clothes basket with my yardstick, stirring her dirty clothes.

What did I expect to turn up? Smells? Memories? I had tried and failed to think up a proper term for moving out day. *Departure* sounds like a ship, *Vacate* like a condemnation order, *Leave* as if she'd been asked to go.

The house groaned with the presence of some element, unseen and unknown, yet as impossible to ignore as a two-headed Cyclops wearing psychedelic helicopter beanies.

As for the weight, the *hazard* of this presence, Jody was oblivious and continued to busily box her products in the bathroom, her bottles of shampoo and conditioner, jars of lotion, scented candles. To refer to the Cyclops would indicate my own awareness of radical change and possibly fear. I said nothing and tried to keep out of her way.

In a rare moment of speculation I'd once bought her that red silk dress. To my knowledge she'd never worn it. It hung on the outside of the closet door, which meant it was the last thing she saw at night. I wondered if she'd take the dress with her.

I went to the butler's pantry and sat down at the table to pay a few bills. Her houseplants were lined up on the radiator cover—a jungle of dieffenbachia, mother-in-law's tongue, Christmas cactus and various vines. In the reflection of the wavy leaded glass window, the same plants appeared as a garden in an impressionist painting.

It seemed I was unable to accept anything at face value, always confounding my thoughts with second guesses and distorting the meaning of what should be clear and simple...a plant should be talked to, watered, and fertilized. Nothing more. Neatly labelled baby food jars contained seedlings that stood no chance of maturing when transplanted to my deeply shaded yard—Cosmos, Zinnias, Chinese forget-me-nots.

Why she persisted in this spring ritual she refused to explain. Sometimes I imagined the attention she lavished on the plants was the baby she'd lost when she was young. When we first became serious, she told me of the event in one short burst. Beyond that, she been unable to continue.

Difficult to remember that licking stamps was no longer necessary. I pressed the stamps on the envelopes and took them to the mailbox. I was the one staying, in my own bungalow, so why did I feel dispossessed?

In all the years we'd lived together she'd never paid a Light, Gas and Water bill. Then again, I'd never asked her. When she offered from time to time, I teased her, said she already contributed by keeping me warm. To share a bed with a woman was more than just sex, though there was an abundance of that, too. I wondered if she'd pack my T-shirt she wore to bed.

I poked my head into the bedroom to check on her progress. After three years together and certain complaints about territorial infringement, I admitted, if only to myself, that I'd actually miss her stuff. Jody, mistress of shoes, had formed in me some sense of her womanhood. Through them I had actually tapped into her essence, her shoes lined up in the closet and around the perimeter of the room, part of an inventory. I imagined them as the feet of the dispossessed, the ones farthest from the closet no longer in favor, a tribe of ghosts left to muddle in solitary confusion and to find something to do, something amusing.

"Fifty-seven pairs of shoes," I said after counting them from my position as Lord of the Manor.

"You exaggerate everything," she said without a care.

Little Ben slapped at a shoestring. With her shoes out of the way, the room would gain square footage, I thought, though Ben would have little to play with. I began folding the bedspread, definitely hers with its swirling black and white design, the sight of which made me slightly tipsy, and placed it in a cellophane bag.

Jody dropped a glass on the bathroom floor, shattering the quiet at the same time Geraldine banged on the screen door. "Yo, glass breakers," she hollered. I blamed my confusion on the bedspread and went to unhook the screen.

She carried a tray of foil-wrapped sandwiches, a jar of Thousand Island dressing and a bowl of potato salad. Though I know she enjoyed verbally joisting with Jody, Geraldine rarely stopped by. Moving day seemed an odd time for a visit.

"Reubens," she announced.

"Is that spelled like the artist?" asked Jody from the bedroom door. Tall, slim, full of grace—she was still as much girl as woman. "If it's not spelled like the artist, I don't want one." Jody was vegetarian, her sandwich sans the corned beef.

"You can't work on an empty stomach."

Geraldine set the food on the refectory table in the dining room, regrettably pushed in small with two chairs—Jody was taking the other four—and somebody, me for instance, would end up eating the same old crow, standing up.

Her red hair sticking up every which-a-way, Geraldine tied on my Tabasco apron. She suggested damp newspaper to pick up the glass and separated a section of morning paper. "It's an old trick," she said and for once Jody didn't disagree. I fetched napkins, bottles of Killian's Red and a stool from the kitchen, spread the food picnic style on the table and sat waiting for what would be my last meal with Jody. Earlier, she'd seemed surprised to find me home.

"I thought you'd stay gone today."

"It's my house," I'd said. "It's where I live."

"It's always been *your* house."

Now Jody carried the sack of glass outside and dropped it into the garbage can. Again, it exploded. I was thinking how glass seems to grow exponentially in volume after it shatters. There seemed to be no end to it.

"Jody, tell me about the new house," said Peg after they'd washed hands and sat down to eat. I knew that Peg had already looked at that house. Peg looked at all mid-town houses up for sale. As a flipper she'd done well, stayed on top of things.

"You get what you pay for. I intend to fix it up."

"Dog of a kitchen," muttered Peg.

"You know I don't cook," said Jody.

Somehow I'd always counted on their antagonism. It gave me ballast. Jody dipped her almost Reuben into the dressing, a stunning shade of coral, for a moment taking me to a sandy beach, blue water and ominous black cliffs in the distance. I imagined us bathing in a lagoon.

"Disreputable bathroom," Peg went on, "but plenty of potential."

"Don't flipper me, Peg," said Jody, as if warning a fish.

"High ceilings, beautiful molding, nice cobalt blue tile inlay in the fireplace. Lofty red oak in the front yard. All in all, lots of potential."

"I could help with the bathroom," I said. "In fact, I could handle the whole renovation."

Both women ignored me.

Geraldine uncapped her potato salad. "Convert to central air as soon as possible. When you're cool you won't get so tired from the hard work. Look, it's a good investment. I was on the verge of buying it myself."

"Thanks for letting me know."

The sauerkraut reminded me I was eating. In the chemistry of change, was a cabbage still a cabbage? Did the vinegar and spice affect its soul?

Jody ate in small bites. Geraldine, often working as well as eating with her male workers, let go of her manners and chomped away as if on break at the job site. She glugged her Killian's from the bottle.

"How will you two divide things?"

Jody shrugged. I looked at the ceiling. She was letting me borrow the two dining chairs which I'd give back after I found replacements. The table was mine to begin with. We'd yet to bring ourselves to discuss ownership of the certain items we'd acquired together: the figurative painting of a man and a woman, arms linked, bodies in opposite direction; an intricate painting of an oxbow lake alive with crows and salamanders; the rarely used brass samovar; her deceased Aunt Jodella's crock of cultured fruit we'd both kept alive; the Peter Songhen pot for our ashes. Jody tried to claim Little Ben, mine to begin with...subject closed.

"He likes me best," she said to no one at all. Little Ben was circling her legs.

"Jody, we've lived together a long time now. Take whatever else you want. The cat stays."

The air was heavy with cat dander. Geraldine dared to speak. "Cat with a little c? Ever notice how you call him *cat* instead of Little Ben?"

"My point exactly," said Jody.

They were in league now and I stood less of a chance. Cat is impersonal, both Jody and Geraldine agreed, and they began talking to each as if they were the animal rescue squad, allied against me.

Geraldine said, "Franko's true feelings for Little Ben are suspect."

"His cat feelings died with Big Ben," offered Jody.

"My *cat*," I reiterated and left the room.

Geraldine finally took her leave and the moving began again. I carried Jody's Shefflera and her Ostrich fern to the U-Haul. She followed with a box top full of the smaller plants she propagates, tiny ferns and African violets.

"Look Franko, we need to discuss what's best for Little Ben. Let's clear the air."

"Sure you want to drive this thing? What if it jack-knifes?"

She glared at me. Her mouth moved. No words came out. I knew I'd said quite enough and committed to silence. We loaded the glider from the front porch. It swung back and forth with our footsteps. I was close to exhaustion, something I'd dealt with since the chemo. In ten years Jody would still look younger, be younger than I was then. I imagined her with a younger muscle, some 30 year-old wonder.

Her clothes I wanted to sniff. Her memorabilia, to touch. Her old crummy furniture, to wax. My chest burned. Instead of taking an ax to everything she owned, smashing and ripping, I sweated and heaved and toted. Violence inside the pit of my stomach swelled to my chest. I was incapable of primitive outbursts, politeness a characteristic.

Otherwise, a slap in the face might have brought me round.

While she packed a box of under garments, I loaded an armful of her shoes, the majority never worn--many called, few chosen--and began my litany: "I offer myself condolences for a life spent on the brink of sex and violence. Salving yourself is part of the game. It's one thing to fall and fall hard, quite another to just stand there teetering on the precipice of danger in a fog of coward's breath."

She pinned up strands of her near-blonde hair. She's not a goddess, just close to it. I continue on. "It's the same as watching a movie when something fearful or alarming is about to happen. Salving yourself is part of the game ... when something fearful or alarming is about to happen, you watch through splayed fingers."

She held up her hand.

"Stop the litany! You're just getting yourself worked up. Not good for your health. If you want to hit me, go ahead. Or for once in your life, just say what you feel. Or try to explain
to me just what you mean. Stop being so Catholic."

"As I recall, you served your time."

She pulled off her work gloves and stuffed them in the back pockets of her jeans. "I'm rehabilitated. Life doesn't have to be a mystery all the time. Why didn't you tell me about your cancer? Why didn't
you tell me yourself?"

"Man, they kept us at it with Fatima," said I, refusing to be pinned down. "The allure of the letter. The great ploy."

"At least you recognize *that*."

"You know I haven't been to church in seventeen years. Do you want the spices?"

She loaded the cumin, coriander, cloves and cayenne pepper into a shoebox. "You can have the Mexican chili powder. I'm taking the plain."

"What about parsley and sage?"

"I'll be growing herbs and flowers. I have a sunny spot."

"You're leaving me because of shade?"

"Dark. You're in the dark."

An inveterate mid-towner, she was moving only a few blocks away. Likely I'd run into her at Zinnie's Or maybe Otherlands. I wouldn't see her at Central Barbecue or Payne's anymore. She only went to those places to accommodate me. She'd order slaw on a bun. I wondered if she'd still flirt with me at the Easy Way, holding up the big tomatoes to her chest or sexually eyeing the bananas or rubbing the cucumbers.

I wondered if on rainy days she'd still sit with me on a bench in Burke's, perusing the used books, talking about the authors. We were both dark as pitch. She wouldn't admit her side of it. Would she wave at me if we cross paths in the Old Forest? And who would *protect* her in the Old Forest?

A painter of oblique birds, Jody didn't consider herself an artist, never said the word *art*. The birds were always black, not just the crows and blackbirds, but all birds. I told her she was afraid of color, afraid to experience gaiety or frivolousness. As if to see through smoke, she squinted at me. "Whose kettle is black here?"

The day crept toward late afternoon. She decided to leave while she still had some hours of daylight. The rest of her belongings she'd pick up later. I was frankly at a loss for words.

Holding herself stiffly, she chose this moment to

stick it to me again. "Look, Franko. So I'm dark. You're dark. Two darks cannot make light."

"Finn's sweater," I said to her. "I left Finn's sweater back in Ireland. Gave it to an old man who was cold. I did it for you."

"The black sweater with the moth holes? The one you stuffed into your suitcase? For me you left out half your underwear and socks ..."

Her pale blue eyes were affixed on mine. She held them there overlong.

I felt certain she could see inside my head. Could she translate the code written there? *Do you love me?* I wanted to say aloud. If you love me, the dark will splinter with a shaft of blinding light, shrivelling death in its golden glow.

Lou Groza

My old man is Charlie Bill Stone. I call him Charlie Bill the same as the rest of his acquaintances down at Alex's where he drinks beer. That's the way he thinks of me, just an acquaintance. My wife, Annie, says stop following him around.

"Search for the *father*," she calls it. "Face up to it. He must have heard she had a baby—must have at least *thought* it might be his."

My mother had an affair with him, but called it quits and soon after married another man. Of my father, she said, "Once he started traveling, he never came around again."

Down at Alex's I sit near him and listen to his stories. I collect each anecdote and seal it into my memory, each word of him. He doesn't know me— the genetic affiliation, that is, and I find the whole secret irresistible—like colorizing an old movie, knowing full well that it ought to be left alone.

He didn't start out selling battery chargers. The job came up along with a freak of nature while he was peddling Rising Sun Flour in and around Memphis. He didn't have to travel any further than Blytheville,

Arkansas, or Greenwood, Mississippi, with the flour. Anyhow, it was then that he ran into Mr. Brock, the Everall man. Mr. Brock saw that he had mechanical ability right away—Charlie Bill jump-started him in a snow storm.

It happened on St. Patrick's Day when everything's supposed to be green. Winter sometimes sits around Memphis doing much of nothing, then, when it's time to move on, shows off with a little going-away party.

Charlie Bill was sitting at the bar in Alex's with some other men when snow started pouring from the sky. It was on a Friday afternoon, and with several rounds of beer downed, Charlie Bill looked out the window and thought the world had lost pigment.

Mr. Brock, the Everall man, was outside, bent over his engine like a polar bear peeking into a cave. The snow had just about covered him.

The antifreeze inside Charlie Bill had settled and he felt the patches of rose-red spreading on his cheeks. His Celtic origin caused him to be more friendly than normal on St. Pat's Day and he zipped up his jacket, opened the door and pressed toward the old man who was fumbling with his battery cables.

"Need some help?" he called into the wind.

Mr. Brock turned his head, neck and shoulders toward him in one motion and mumbled through his frozen lips. He was testy with cold, his eyelashes stiff with ice. "Doubt you can do anything." His words rolled out like snowballs.

Charlie Bill pointed toward his rattletrap Ford parked next to the old man's brand-new Chevrolet Station Wagon.

"Jumper cables," he said.

He'd learned the hard way about missing an appointment because of a dead battery. Lost a sizable order for Rising Sun from Harts Bakery. For the most part, it pays to be helpful. He got the station wagon started and Mr. Brock offered him a job selling Everalls. As it turned out, the old man was nearing retirement and looking for "a good man to know." He trained Charlie Bill, they split commission, then some years later Charlie Bill took over the territory. "You reap what you sow," but whenever he says this I wonder if it's true.

Because of the sudden snow storm, Charlie Bill busted around the South for some thirty-five years, the same as an old-time traveling medicine man, but instead of Wofford's Elixir or Abraham's Tonic, he sold the Everall. Sassy—that's what he calls my mother, though I never heard her called anything but Sarah—had wanted him to stick with Rising Sun and closer to home, but Charlie Bill could not ignore an opportunity when it stared him full in the face. He'd grown up wearing one of two pair of white socks. There was a big world out there with a lot of dead batteries in it.

Apparently this was the time when they became disenchanted with each other and split—*him* because he refused to be held down by a woman, *her* because she wasn't about to sit home while he roamed free, neither of them knowing that *I* was already a zygote.

Mr. Brock taught him the business with the patience of a mule driver. He shared the wisdom gotten from thirty years of road travel and spit out enough evangelism to save Charlie Bill and maybe four or five other traveling men from the wickedness ready and waiting in each motel and roadhouse.

Charlie Bill copied Mr. Brock like a shadow and from him learned "the four Ps'" — *Persistence, Pressure, Praise, and Presentation*. Charlie Bill kept his nose clean, his eyes on the road, and soon he drove a brand-new gray Ford station wagon loaded down with black Everalls, their red and white knobs lined up dress-right-dress, the hard work of selling made a lot easier by equipment that appeared able to do the job. Charlie Bill peddled battery chargers all over hell and half of Georgia—hardly ever came back home with one. A station wagon might not paint the same picture of prosperity as say, a Buick Sedan, but it held a whole damn squadron of Everalls.

Back then Charlie Bill was almost a "homing pigeon," though he spent more time at Alex's than his rooming house, the same as he does now. He would leave the rented room at the beginning of each week, Sunday on his calendar, and travel straight through until Friday when he landed back at Alex's, which is where he is now. Where I am.

I'm on sabbatical from the university and have sat here a portion of each day for the last five weeks. Fate led me into the place — I stopped in for a beer after a day of research at the library.

Annie doesn't believe in accident — "You've been tip-toeing around him for years," she said. "Now that you know who he is, why not confront him and get it over with."

Mourning for a father I didn't know was a part of me, like body hair, and I wasn't about to shave it off so abruptly. Sadness, the bulk and weight of it, was what formed me, the essential ingredient of my wonder years.

At any rate, regulars in Alex's sidle up and, as part of the ritual, make some comment about the weather, never seeming to notice that it's the same in a bar day in and day out, and then introduce themselves. When the old man said "Charlie Bill Stone" and stuck his hand out, I said "Charles Wilson Moran," smiled broadly to keep my lips from trembling, and shook hands with him. If he knew the connection between us his face never showed it. In a menopausal funk, my mother had admitted the whole truth — that I was not the product of Wilson Moran, the grocer, but of Charlie Bill Stone, the wandering gypsy, the very thing that drove Wilson Moran to divorce her. He wasn't about to raise another man's wild oats.

"Priceless shit," was Annie's jab.

At Alex's they give everyone a nickname and since I teach history, they quickly dubbed me "Professor." The title seems somewhat ludicrous for a grown man attempting to climb a greased pole, but I say to myself, *Hold on there*.

Annie insists that my study of history supplants my real need to find my own origins. Quite possible, I tell her.

"A knee grown from shallow roots of a cypress tree in a swamp glazed with green slime" is the way I like to put it. She moans, shakes her head and says I'm bound to slip in my own shit. Annie wouldn't like my saying it, but she talks much the same as my mother.

Marikoes stands Charlie Bill a round of beer and lays his quarters out on the table. Always the bus ride makes Charlie Bill tense and now he unwinds like a spool of thread. He puts two of Marikoes' quarters in the juke box and presses "It's All in the Game." He sips his beer and waits for Marikoes to make two more selections.

In this gathering of old men, the past flows into the present where it stands stagnant. I navigate Charlie Bill's past without a map, wondering what I will bump into.

"So what's happening out in the world, C.B.?" Marikoes most always begins their conversations this way.

"Armadillos," says Charlie Bill. "They've walked up from Texas. See 'um all over Mississippi now. I ran over one last time I was on the road."

Ten years ago, I'm thinking from my perch on the bar stool as I watch his faraway look, *it's been ten years since you flattened the armadillo.*

Marikoes nods and hunches his shoulders, sliding his finger down the list of songs.

Out there on the road, Charlie Bill saw many a peculiar sight; his list of wild animals caged out back of gas stations includes bears, snakes, deer, and llamas. But no armadillos. "People would stop and feed the animals scraps they wouldn't give an old dog," he says. "I'd always be tempted to open the cage and let the animals go."

From behind the bar Ernestine offers her opinion. "The owners had to make a buck somehow, now didn't they? Everybody does. Life's hard." The hard lines of Ernestine's face under the wiry tufts of gray hair show the truth of her statement.

I reach for the peanuts on the bar and imagine myself and Ernestine as animals running through the gate and into the woods. Set free by Charlie Bill.

Marikoes chooses "Alfie" and another tune that he calls a surprise.

"Alfie" makes me think of the marriage I stepped away from," says Charlie Bill, and I am listening hard now. He almost never mentions her, and rarely by name, but I wait for it to come. Instead he skips over to music, one of his favorite topics.

"Times have changed, even here in Alex's. The music on the juke box used to be the best in the city. For all I know, it still is. Not much rock—and, for God sakes, not much of the fitful twanging from Nashville. Out on the road you can't get much else."

Marikoes' surprise tune sounds like the ocean. "New Wave," he says, and smiles at me in conspiracy that says that he's old in years but young at heart. He's hard pressed to keep up with his own wise-looking Greek face and I smile back as if he were one of my less gifted students who needs assurance.

Charlie Bill's short-term memory isn't much good. "What kind of music?"

"New Wave. It's like being in a dream, C.B."

Charlie Bill loads the quarters and punches

"Have You Met Miss Jones?" and "Porgy" and "The Memphis Blues" and waits for the dream to end.

"They'll change all this to compact discs soon," I tell them. "You won't be able to buy records and tapes much longer."

"Everything changes," says Charlie Bill. "Up until 1977 you could only get burgers with lettuce, tomato, and mayo in here. Then *everybody*–but Lazarus—got into health."

Charlie Bill looks over at Ernestine behind the bar and says, "Give me a low fat cottage cheese, Ernestine. Hold the peach." He looks over at me, then at Marikoes across from him in the booth. "People try to give you fruit whether you have a tolerance for it or not."

"It's the fat content now," I interject from my stool. "Grams."

"Yeah. I heard that," he says. He looks at me and draws on the beer. "I guess I'd better keep account of all that, Professor."

Even if he could stretch out the curvature of his stoop, I am taller by several inches. Probably his mottled gray hair once looked sandy red the same as my own. Our eyes are blue. Forcing him into the present seems unacceptable and I wish I'd held back, fully understanding that more time must pass before I approach him with the news. I am a patient historian grubbing for my own history. Annie says, "Stop worrying over who fucked who when and get on with your life. He's an old worn-out wagon jobber. Low-life, about like your mother."

Annie's a sharp saw. But it's not so bad when you expect it, *know* it's coming.

Lazarus sits rigidly at the far end of the bar as if rigor mortis had set in. He's the only one of the regulars who still smokes. He resents the imposed isolation and puffs earnestly to get even.

Ernestine gets the salad out of the cooler and takes off the plastic wrap. She cuts carrots in julienne strips and arranges them like a stack of firewood alongside the greens, then walks over and sets it in front of Charlie Bill. He munches the cucumbers, then quickly swallow a forkful of the cottage cheese, avoiding the taste.

"At least the furniture's still original," he says, looking at the barstools in my direction. "When they'd get rickety, Alex would just get out his auger and go at it. That's why they've lasted so long. Now the boy here does the fixing."

Alex, Jr., busily dries glasses and gives Charlie Bill the gift of his handsome smile. "Yeah. Yeah."

"Big Alex would be proud of you, kid," says Marikoes.

Kid repeats in my head. Alex, Jr. and I are about

the same age. I imagine us as boys playing together at the foot of the shuffleboard table, sifting sand, throwing it in each other's eyes.

Alex's Bar and Grill, along with the Sports Club where Charlie Bill takes a steam, are solid establishments. "The best," he says. Other places just come and go. Above all, he is faithful to these places. I covet his sense of place and order a hamburger with lettuce, tomato, and mayo.

"Hold the peach," I hear myself say.

"Don't come with no peach," says Ernestine, setting me straight.

Lonnie the blind broom man taps his way through the door and into the bar, marking his steps. Charlie Bill cuts the lettuce with the side of his fork, but looks up when Lonnie comes alongside the booth. "Mr. Lonnie, you not speaking today?"

Lonnie stops and gets his bearing. "When's your birthday?"

"Born on April the second, nineteen and twenty-five," says Charlie Bill. "Just missed being a fool," and I wait to hear him say "No fool like an old fool," and he does.

Then Lonnie tells what day of the week Charlie Bill was born—Friday—a demonstration of his specialty. Charlie Bill buys a broom in appreciation and then gives it to Alex, Jr. Over the past five weeks,

Charlie Bill has bought three brooms in what seems a kind of religious obligation. I envision bundles of brooms clustered in the corners of Charlie Bill's rented room, the affirmation of his faith, hope, and charity.

Suddenly, I want a cake, one that is frosted with new-fallen snow. I want to tell Lonnie my own date of birth. July third, nineteen fifty-one! I want Charlie Bill to listen up—just be struck by it like the head of a blazing match, then quietly buy a broom and present it to me.

"So tell me about your heritage," I ask Marikoes just to get rid of the birthday blues. Jab a can full of holes and it sinks quickly. Marikoes starts up about the beauty and solemnity of the Greek Orthodox Church. His memories all seem to center on his childhood and I am certain he hasn't set foot in church for many years.

Lazarus coughs on his own smoke. He resents the talk of Christians. "They bring up the religion just to taunt me," he says to Ernestine.

"Quit sulking," she says. "I've never held you personally responsible."

Charlie Bill says that the closest he's gotten to a church in years is the summer night revivals he sat through out on the road for lack of something better to do.

"I never was visited by Jesus like Mr. Bock, mind

you, but my ears got reamed out a time or two by the preachers." He says he can still hear Reverend Moon's thunder. '"And I say unto you, the man who fornicates with the Devil today will lie in a bed of hot coal tomorrow!"'

He tells this story to Marikoes who doesn't mention that he's heard it before. On that night, at the revival, Charlie Bill took a good look at the people around him who were listening to Moon, trailer people, dirt farmers and down-and-outers, just out lookin' for a comfortable place to sit for a while and air themselves.

The people squirmed in the heat, and inspired by the bellowing Reverend Moon, they poured fervor and one by one declared for Jesus.

Charlie Bill saved himself from religion by imagining that he was at a football game. When the lot of them stood up and hollered for Jesus, Charlie Bill got up and cheered for Lou Groza as if he'd just kicked a field goal.

Cubby Bear Callan walks through the door and slides into Charlie Bill's booth as easily as a hand into a glove. "Hi, Fossils," he says and then nods toward me. "Afternoon, Professor."

Cubby looks as friendly as a little bright-eyed stuffed animal a child might carry around and I wave to him. When first I started this venture, I figured on quick satiation, then walk away forever. Now I feel as if I were looking down from the middle rung of a ladder, in danger of falling in with them and not able to get back up.

Charlie Bill looks faraway as if he's still out on the road. Alex, Jr. brings a bowl of redskins and sets it on the table, and Charlie Bill tells the story about the monument to the Boll Weevil in Enterprise, Alabama, and how the insect ruined the cotton crop and the farmers got rich planting peanuts instead.

Cubby steadily pops the redskins into his mouth.

"C.B., you miss the gypsy life?"

"I've seen it all, don't want to see more," says Charlie Bill, moving the nuts away from Cubby. "Not even if they'd give my driver's license back. I stayed on the road way too long, but I had to save money for his college."

"College" tackles me hard and I struggle to get back up. She always told me *she'd* saved it, little by little, from the job at Kress's. Sometimes I wondered if she'd gotten the money from the men who came and went, and now I feel relief.

"I never was sure if he got any of it, mind you." Charlie Bill looks into his beer. "Later, I stopped sending. I figured if they were hard up, she'd let me know soon enough."

Lonnie works birthdays and brooms at the bar.

"Mathematical formula's not fair when it comes to you, baby boy!" says Lonnie to Alex, Jr., in a resonant voice that startles me each time I hear it, expecting instead a muffled sound to go along with the blurred eyes. "Your old man passed out Havana Coronas on that day. Nobody could forget!"

Ronnie Rosemary ambles through the back door and sits on a stool between me and Lazarus. Ronnie's an old mongoloid who has outlived almost every other one of his kind born in his generation, but even Ronnie seems to remember the day of Alex, Jr.'s birth. He mumbles and pretends to smoke an imaginary Havana Corona.

"The line's three and a half for the Bear-Giants game Saturday," says Cubby, tired of random conversation. He wants to land on sports and stay there. He pulls a pad and pencil from his shirt pocket, ready to take bets.

Charlie Bill recalls the fried gizzards they ate during the football games prior to the days of their good health. "Lou Groza was my main man back then," he says. "And old Alex was second. He did the frying." Young Alex now continues the tradition, except he does buffalo wings.

"If we could just put that mind of yours to better use, Mr. Lonnie," says Marikoes. "C'mon. Figure out the Giant's game Saturday."

"I don't bet on what I can't see," says Lonnie.

"What about the birthdays?" asks Charlie Bill.

"That's a sure thing. The writing's on the wall right in here." He knocks on his own head and smiles. His eyes roll all over hell and back.

Ronnie Rosemary spins himself around on the bar stool until he's dizzy, stares into the mirror for a few seconds, then closes his eyes and rests.

"He's daydreaming," says Charlie Bill. "Okay for him, but regular people have to fight against daydreams, especially out on the road. Daydreams turn the brain to grits. Out there I'd try to remember the name of every person I knew in a certain town. Mobile was hard—I knew fifty people there, but in burgs like Pontotoc, Lucedale, and Brownsville it was a snap. Sometimes I'd spell words backwards, or count cars with northern license plates. Anything to stay alert."

I pick up a handful of redskins and pop one into my mouth, and pass the bowl to Ronnie. I sit there and wonder what it would be like to walk around in a daze like Ronnie, eating nuts and daydreaming. No future. No past. Only the present.

"The one thing I daydreamed about was coming home and watching the Cleveland Browns on the TV. Always I'd buy peanuts in Enterprise and save some for the game. But when Lou came onto the field I'd put down the Schmidt and park the nuts."

"Schmidt," grumbles Lazarus. "*It* freezes before the *milk* does."

Charlie Bill looks at me. "Make sure Ronnie chews one nut at a time," and he continues his story. "The ball snaps, then Lou takes his strides, then whop—he kicks and the pigskin flies like an eagle." He raises his shoulders and his voice. Every one takes the cue and nods, even Lazarus. "Like watching hope," says Charlie Bill. He takes a long draw on the beer.

"Confidence," he says. "That was Lou. Whenever sales were down, I talked about Lou's toe. 'Steady as Lou's toe,' I'd say, or turn it around—'his toe is as steady and reliable as the Everall.' Not exactly true, of course. Groza never missed, but the Everall was not entirely problem free—I figured that one out right off when Mr. Brock's battery went dead and with him cussing about having left it on charge all night."

Charlie Bill stiffens. "Mr. Brock was not all the time reliable either. One such time he got things mixed up and sent me off to a sales meeting. When I got to this building way out in the boonies, it was empty. Not one soul in there. That's when I split with Sassy. I got home earlier than she thought and caught her with this guy. Sometimes I think the building was an omen."

I imagine my mother entwined with her lover, not hearing the door creak when Charlie Bill comes into her lair and discovers them, then Charlie Bill as he runs to the car, guns the motor and roars out on the road, never looking back, while I, the zygote, lie helpless inside her as she disgraces us both.

Witness to her sin, I squirm to tell him. Sarah Moran, I say to myself and right then I know what Annie would say—You keep counsel with your own ass because you can't bear to admit your mother's a disgraceful bitch. Tell him. I embrace Annie's wisdom, my sweet and sour Annie, and right out loud say, "Sarah Moran."

Stunned, Charlie Bill's eyes widen and brim under a furrowed brow, and he suddenly begins a recitation of Lou Groza's statistics, starting with the late forties and steadily elevating his voice as he moves through the fifties, but stops abruptly in "nineteen and sixty-one" when Ronnie lights the cigar given to him by Lazarus.

"Hey, Ronnie's not supposed to smoke."

"He's grown, ain't he? He deserves some pleasure."

Everyone glares at Lazarus.

"Oh, all right," he says and takes back the cigar. He gives Ronnie an Evergreen Lifesaver instead.

Charlie Bill turns back to the subject of Groza.

"No getting around it, of course. Lou had it all over a guy like me. Never was much chance in Lou taking one in the groin. Big Bubbas were out there fronting for him." He looks toward me now and throws his voice in my direction. "In real life, nobody blocks for you. You take it in the gut. Keep hold of your confidence, stay with it and be prepared. That's the trick. It's like a black bird up there on a wire, minding his own business—you never know when the current might shock you. The hot seat. But you take it and go on."

Cubby Bear, Marikoes, and Lonnie all nod grimly behind the cloud of Lazarus's smoke. Ernestine quits wiping the counter and leans on the cash register. Looking at me, she takes a deep breath. "I think this pertains to you, Peaches. It don't have nothing to do with no Cleveland Browns."

Charlie Bill puts his cap back on, as if afraid what's on his mind might escape before he talks it out properly. "Before he retired, Lou was one of the oldest players in pro ball. He kept at it. If anything you should admire a man sticking to his life's work."

He looks at the ceiling and back down again at me.

"At one time I saw the numbers running up the odometer as money in the bank. I thought I'd marry and raise a couple of kids, buy a little house and pay for it body and soul the same as everybody else, but it didn't work out. Anyhow, nobody, I don't guess, ever gets done with the paying."

"That's true," I assure him, then lapse into silence. He's unrolling. I give him room for his scroll.

"The American dream was the reason for living out of a suitcase, eating artificial food and sleeping in the green and gold motel rooms at the Holiday Inn. And after things went bad, riding the highways flattened out the hard lumps and kept them from piling up again. I missed out on that house though," he said. "Most likely Sassy would have decorated the damn thing gold and olive green anyhow, same as the motel rooms. Every traveling man back then said the same thing. Green and gold. Even in the most expensive rooms. Even Lou Groza's, I bet. Every one of them the same."

Charlie Bill orders a large pitcher, then looks at Cubby.

"Might as well get the big one. You're gonna drink half of it anyhow. Beats me how a man not much bigger than a midget can hold more beer than a giant."

"As much as Lou Groza," says Marikoes. "As much as the whole damn Cleveland squad."

Cubby's little red face lights with pride.

"I guess the Browns gave up booze during the

season," I suggest to Charlie Bill.

"Oh, yeah. Booze will kill you in the season."

I can wait no longer. Straddling a narrow chasm, I fall in. "Charlie Bill," I say to him. "Who's your next of kin?"

Through the bottom of the glass cross-cross lines over his face suggest infirmity. He moves his lips, groping for an answer.

"For Christ's sake," says Marikoes out of the side of his mouth. "His next of kin's Lou Groza!"

"Lou Groza, he's Italian," says Cubby. "C.B.'s not Italian."

"Thank God," says Lazarus.

I am the place-kicker, alone on the bench waiting for the fourth down. Then Charlie Bill looks over at me and straightaway his face brightens. He motions Cubby to sit by Marikoes.

And then it's my turn. I slide off of the stool and move toward his booth, stumbling clumsily, and take my seat beside him.

His elbow pokes in my ribs.

"He's Groza."

"Groza," I repeat, my wild son-of-a-gypsy heart pounding. The scattered sorrow mounds in place. Inside my head I hear Annie's words sawing to the heart of things and I hope she keeps counsel with herself. That she doesn't cut too deep.

The Things She Carries

In the fall of 1963, he called her out of the blue. When she heard his voice on the phone, the words got caught in her throat—she was barely able to speak to him, and after the long silence, he asked to meet her in Overton Park at the old octagonal pavilion.

She was twenty-one and married, with a one year old son. She borrowed her mother's car, plus her mother agreed to watch the baby.

"Doctor's appointment," she told her mother, the lie sticky in her throat.

Her mother had bought the immaculate blue Chrysler Imperial from an old spinster and kept it in that same showroom condition as if inherited, the ASH RECEIVER spotless, the leather seats supple, the polished chrome dazzling. The parched yellowed warning signs and operating instructions were still affixed to the visors.

She was shaking inside as she drove her mother's precious car through the streets and into the park. The car was a grand coach when what she really needed was to walk on solid ground to steady herself.

She parked near the green pavilion and sat waiting in the car, looking at her watch, rewinding it, then lit a cigarette. Not to sully the ASH RECEIVER, she flicked the ashes out the vent window.

A car with an out-of-state license plate drove into the lot on the opposite side of the pavilion. He got out, his brilliant form ramrod straight. The car then sped away, spewing gravel. He came around the pavilion, his black shoes military issue, his clothes civilian, as if between two worlds. He stood beside the passenger's side of the car for a moment—her heart was beating hard in her chest. He opened the door and got in. They both looked down, afraid for their eyes to meet.

He glanced around the car and smiled by the hardest. He read the instructions aloud. "FASTEN SEAT BELTS. INSERT KEY IN IGNITION. You probably need the reminders. Among other things, you promised never to smoke. I guess you forgot that, too."

She muttered something she no longer remembers. The heavy air ballooned in her chest. She could hear herself breathing, feel the balloon expanding.

"Let's walk," he said, and they both got out of the car.

She blew the smoke away from him, then dropped the cigarette on the ground and mashed it. They walked toward the pavilion, the pebbles crunching underfoot. The Old Forest was yielding to fall, the dogwoods red, the hickories bright yellow, the oaks brown. Thick runaway vines grew up a giant Sherman oak, a woodpecker drilled the bark for bugs, the squirrels chasing in the branches.

They walked up the pavilion steps littered with acorns, and slowly circled the perimeter, working through the silence.

Finally they stood still. Where the pavilion post joined the ceiling, a spider tatted its fan-shaped web, a small world of its own making, the pattern of silver threads strong and enduring.

He leaned against the railing. "Doesn't he feed you?"

"You're thin, too."

He'd been an Army weapons expert on a secret mission to train dirt-poor farmers in Laos to fight the Communists. Nobody was supposed to know about American involvement there. His was a secret mission. From various parts of Europe, France mostly, his unit was flown to Laos and dropped into the jungle. He was never sure of his exact location. He trained the farmers who knew nothing of guns to break down sophisticated weapons and to clean them. He trained them to shoot to kill. But he could not train them to win against all odds, and he knew, as he labored to communicate with them in French and with hand signals, that most of them would soon die.

He would not talk to her about his wounds, or how long it took to recover from them. She suspected he never would. He said, "A little shrapnel in the head is all. They told me to stay away from magnets."

Had things turned out differently, she was to receive his personal effects. He stared at her when he said it, the light in his green eyes dulled by the face of death, by what he'd seen and done. She wanted very much to look away, but endured his eyes, knowing she might never see him again.

He said, "I had this image of your face when you opened the package. I don't know if I wanted to let you know I loved you or to hurt you bad."

He stood up straight, placed a small pouch in her hand and wrapped her fingers around it. "Thinking about you kept me alive. These belong to you."

Abruptly, he steered her down the steps and across the gravel to the car and opened the door. Her eyes wandered his face, soaked him in, the male part of her never tested in battle. At that moment she wanted nothing more of life than to hold him in her arms.

"Motherhood so becomes you," he said, swallowing hard.

The car that brought him pulled into the lot and idled, the driver a woman with blonde hair.

He said, "If you ever need me, no matter where you are or who you're with or what you've done, I'll come to you."

Squirrels chattered in the trees, the blue jays screaming. He touched her hair and she closed her eyes, and when she reached for him, he was gone.

Time crackles, as if burning. Years after the Vietnam War was over, she received his poems. In verse he'd travelled back to the Ragged Edge of Time, as he called it, where he struggled to end his own war.

The little Laotian girl, Su Lei, was a five-year-old orphan with coal black hair and a huge bright smile. Her black eyes were lights in the midst of an impoverished village battered by war and deceit. From the door of a tarpaper hut, she watched him — the tall man, the tallest she'd ever seen — instruct the men of her village. Even the wise elders, who knew everything there was to know, gathered to listen.

She'd follow him around the village, tugging on his fatigue jacket and shyly presenting him with wildflowers — Jimson weed or Horse Nettle, her hands hiding her face when he teased her.

In the light from the cook fire that shone against a dirt mound, he made shadow art with his hands — silhouettes of rabbits and coyotes and cows. She learned to sing *Frère Jacques*, *Old Paint* and *Blue Bayou*. He gave her a pencil and pad, taught her to print Su Lei and U.S.A. "U.S. is us," he told her — and he hoped to bring her to America, to educate and to raise her.

He took some of the men on a training mission, advancing miles from the village. It was hot that day, a glassy haze over fields boiling with birds, the men slow-moving through grasses and trees, until suddenly they crossed a muddy stream and encountered an enemy cadre. A quick skirmish, rapid fire, and it was done. The men swaggered a little as they turned homeward.

Halfway back to the village the smoke in the distance sent them running. Huts burning. Fields afire. Men, women, and children, raped and shot — corpses everywhere, the wounded crying out. A few yards from the huts he found her maimed body covered in blood, her hair matted in dirt, U.S. printed on the crumpled paper spilt from her hand like a stone. The fallen sky muffled sound.

He raged against himself for her suffering, against the enemy for cowardice, against God for not protecting her. With a purpose as hard as granite, he killed her enemies — a rampage — dozens of them shot through the heart, until he lost himself, until he felt nothing.

In her recurring dream, she receives the special

delivery package, signs her name, then stares at the brown paper wrapping, running her fingers along the rough twine, afraid to look inside, afraid to see his watch, his dog tags, his medals. His blood and bones.

When finally she opens the package, it contains nothing, and she wakes, touching her throat, swallowing the night. Somewhere in the world, he is alive, breathing the same air she breathes.

She hid the pouch containing his medals on the bookshelf in her small study, first behind *The Red Badge of Courage*, then later *The Things They Carried*. Sometimes she slips the medals out of the pouch and stares at them in the palm of her hand. Sometimes she pins them to her bra, sometimes carries them in her pocket. The heft of them slows her movements. When she dies, she wonders what will they say about the medals: her Purple Heart and her Bronze Star.

Banana Day

I was twelve years old when *My Babe* came pumping out of the radio. Our parents had allowed my older brother John to move the radio-record player combo from the living room into his room so they wouldn't have to hear his music late at night. I couldn't hear it either, so I'd slip out of bed and crouch outside his door to listen.

On Red, Hot, & Blue — "the hottest thing in the country" — Daddy-O Dewey Phillips sold Falstaff Beer . . . "If you can't drink it, open up a rib and pour it in." He'd play Little Richard and Sister Rosetta Tharpe. He'd play "Blue Suede Shoes." He'd play "Heartbreak Hotel" twenty times in a row. He'd play Howlin' Wolf and Billy Lee Riley. He'd play "Tell Me Why You Like Roosevelt."

I'd toast my fingers over the floor furnace grate, still a little warm, and hope not to be discovered. I doubted John would ever make good his threat to knock the breath out of me for pestering him — he'd never hit a girl — but I didn't want to test him and maybe spoil things for our parents who thought he'd end up as a priest. Our family needed to produce a priest — or better still, a saint — to make up for the sins of Uncle Jim Kinnane. The first time I heard the bone rattling music, I knew it wouldn't be me.

After school while John was at football practice, I was allowed to go in there and play the few forty-five records I owned, the ones I'd first heard on *Red, Hot, & Blue*.

"Old Joe-Joe Da-Coogie," Dewey would say. "Go on down and tell him Phillips sentcha."

Coughi's Pop Tunes Record Shop didn't yet have "My Babe." "On order," the clerk said time and again after I'd walked a mile to the store.

Days passed, still the record didn't come, and finally in desperation I caught the bus downtown. The bus turned onto Main Street. My head was sweating, my hair slick to the touch as if coated with Vaseline. My parents allowed me to ride no farther south than Goldsmith's Department Store—blocks shy of Beale—and obediently I got off at that stop.

They'd said nothing about walking, and with a sense of fear and wonder I started toward Beale Street where our notorious ancestor had owned the Monarch Saloon—the most famous Colored saloon in the South, my father had called it, my mother quickly cautioning him not to romanticize Uncle Jim and the *other* record store Dewey advertised—Home of the Blues—down on forbidden Beale Street.

The late afternoon sun cropped the buildings on

Beale Street, leaving a tunnel of blue shade. The storefront windows reflected my own green suede loafers, step by green step. I passed Lansky's where Elvis bought his clothes, Schwab's Sundry Store known for potions and charms, and the One-Minute Café famous for chili dogs. For the most part the street was boarded up and deserted. Gone dry, as W.C. Handy put it.

I entered the Home of the Blues, tripping at the threshold, and immediately endured as best I could the sharp stare of an old white-bearded, mahogany-skinned man behind the cash register. The other customers and clerks, all of them black, were staring at me, too.

Nervously I glanced over the display bins, hoping to quickly find the record without asking for help. To speak would mean my voice might crack like a boy's.

"You want something?"

The grumpy old man's chiselled frown told me, in no uncertain terms, that he wanted me out of his store. If he'd seen me coming in the first place, he'd have locked the door and placed the CLOSED sign in the window.

I was scared to death — that because I was white — he wouldn't sell me the record, or he'd try to gyp me with the Pat Boone version.

I took a deep breath and stared back at the man, my face hot as fire, my eyes burning. I was not leaving the store without the record.

"*My Babe* by Marion 'Little Walter' Jacobs." I said it barely above a whisper in a voice as transparent as cellophane. At least I wasn't yellow.

He frowned back at me, motioned me to the counter, then slid *My Babe* into a brown paper sack. "Now don't be coming 'round here no more."

I paid for the record, my hand fumbling the change, and I had difficulty picking up the coins with my short, bitten nails. Without counting it, I left the store, clutching the sack to my chest, and headed farther down Beale Street. Reportedly, Uncle Jim had loved Colored ways, and maybe I'd taken after him, black music under my skin the way it had gotten under his. I spotted the carved stone Venetian window above the cast-iron storefront of 340 Beale where Uncle Jim had operated his sin and gambling den, where W.C. Handy had lifted the piano riffs of Bennie Frenchie and set them down in the *St. Louis Blues*, and where Jelly Roll Morton—playin' the dozens, wearing shoes fixed with flashing light bulbs—had poked fun at Frenchie's style and lived to tell about it . . . lucky for him when you consider the nickname of the Monarch Saloon—the Castle of the Missing Men. I stood before the padlocked building, wanting very badly to go inside. If I'd lived in Uncle Jim's era and entered the saloon, I knew very well that he, too, would have told me not to come 'round here ever again. When I arrived home, Lena was still there, finishing up the week's ironing. I told Lena what I'd done. She frowned and said, "Baby, Beale Street ain't no fitting place for you. This family has had a hard enough time living down Mr. Jim."

***

I end my writing session for the day. For tomorrow's session I sharpen three #2 pencils — Father, Son, Holy Ghost — taking each one down an eighth of an inch, the grinding irrational since I now use a word processor. I read over the work of the past several weeks, the seams of the story blurred now, and I find myself unable to separate fact from fiction. For many generations my family has lived in Memphis — so many generations, in fact, that the city seems to live within my head. I wander the streets where memories meet dreams, the illusion more real to me than life itself. I stack the pages of my story and set them on the desk.

Falstaff beer pops back into my head. You stop writing for the day, but you don't stop thinking. I'm remembering BD and me taking the Sante Fe Chief to Flagstaff, Arizona, driving to the Grand Canyon, and riding mules to the bottom of the canyon floor . . . I'm scared the whole time because I don't like heights, and I look toward the interior canyon wall most of the way down. I'm talking hours! The switchbacks are murder, and I hug that mule when we get to the bottom—Shoofly was his name—and I hug him again when we get back safely to the top.

On the drive back to Flagstaff, BD insists on buying me a beer—he's a liver transplantee and no longer drinks alcohol, but he remembers beer with affection.

"I don't want a beer," I tell him.

He says, "Yeah, yeah you do," and he pulls up to a convenience store.

"I don't want a beer."

I hate repeating myself, and he knows it . . . we've been married a million years. I'm beginning to get hot under the collar. I know he's just as stiff and sore as I am, plus it's been a long day and he gets sleepy behind the wheel. He knows good and well he can count on me.

"I'll spell you," I tell him, talking cowgirl talk.

He says, "No, you just relax. Have a cold one."

I burn a hole in his cheek staring until he turns to face me, then inhale deeply to get my voice pumped up. "I'll have a beer when and if we get to Falstaff!"

A ringing noise startles me, and for a moment I think it's the little house wren outside my window, in a change of key.

I run to the kitchen, catch the phone on the fourth ring, and hear the drawling voice of my cousin Guy Bean, his call as rare as a blue moon. I'm hoping the subject is money, which he owes me. His mother is my favorite aunt, the reason I still speak to him at all. Guy says *Maw*grit the same way Aunt Roux does, and I let him into my head.

"Hold on," he says, and I wonder why he chose this moment to call me in the first place. It would be just like him to let me cool my heels while he scrambles his eggs or butters his toast.

I click on the radio—WKLR—and hear Captain Pete's smoky voice. He spins Muddy Waters' *Mannish Boy*, and with the receiver held to my ear, I drum my fingers on the top of my head and tap my heel.

Guy is an artist who can paint just about anything. He copies works of famous impressionist painters and signs them Guy Manet, or Guy Degas, or Guy Prendegast. He sells his paintings to commercial establishments, mostly bars and restaurants. In dimly lit areas, you'd think they were the originals.

I'm keen on his paintings of rural southern life, especially his red-eyed, bucktoothed mules so alive they seem to bray. The owner of the Half Shell Restaurant bought a whole troop of Guy's mules.

When you sit in his place eating gumbo and

drinking beer, you'd swear you were in an auction barn. Mostly, Guy pays his bills—when he pays them—by painting portraits. Sometimes he'll paint the portrait of a celebrity from a publicity photograph, then   present the portrait to the celeb—along with the bill—as if he'd been commissioned for the work all along.

Some of the celebs have Guy thrown out—Whitney Houston, for example—while others, such as Mohammed Ali and Willie Nelson, admire his moxie, along with his skill, and commission him for more work.

Guy finally comes back to the phone. He talks real slow, allowing two words at a time—"Mawgrit, I want . . . to do . . . your portrait." It's a group wedding, and I lean on the kitchen counter and wait for his couples to come down the aisle and marry. I am fifty-something years old and thinking *why now?*

"I need a photograph to work with. Come on over and I'll shoot you." He laughs at his own joke, a sort of underground laugh.

I walk toward the kitchen window stretching the coiled telephone cord taut the same way he'd done each coil of my corkscrewed hair at a family celebration when I was six, he seven. My mother, who had worked all morning to make me presentable, never quite forgave him. I run my tongue over my front teeth and think about his mules. When I was a child, braces were not an option unless the front teeth protruded to the extreme. I push back the long bill of my black baseball cap, then roll up the sleeves of my ragged work shirt and the cuffs of my shorts, wishing I'd had my eyelids lifted.

"I'm not dressed for it."

"Mawgrit, fix up and come on. I'll make you look thirty-five again. It won't cost you a dime."

Today I'm planning to build a retaining wall. Outside, clasped over the top of the fence where I left them yesterday, my work gloves appear to be the green fingers of someone pulling up from the other side.

The neighbor's cat, Cornbob, creeps through the grass toward the huge pallet of stones set down at the end of the washed-gravel driveway by the delivery man in his truck equipped with the hydraulic lift. The stones are genuine river stones washed a million times over in an Arkansas stream, stones that were shaped by the water itself.

Without hesitation I chose them over the fieldstones.

Maybe Guy's dormant conscience has finally awakened. Maybe he wants to retire his old debt to my late father by painting me. I picture my two brothers, John and James—THE FINN BROTHERS it says on the side of John's truck—working away in the *New California* where they fix chimneys undermined by the shifting terrain. John is the tallest as well as the oldest, which rankles James.

Both of them have big Finn butts. John wears overalls, James cat-black pants. If my brothers knew about Guy's proposal, their derisive laughter—like a weather siren—might keep me at home. For God's sake, don't give him any money! But neither of them is ever around when needed.

I pat my fanny and wonder if the twenty miles of power-walking per week, plus two gruelling sessions of kick-boxing is worth the effort.

On the other end of the phone Guy is steadily crunching something. An apple, or a carrot. He clears his throat. "What I'm doing is a series of portraits of Memphis writers. Shelby Foote for one . . . you for another . . . "

Inside his long pause is the ground I am about to give up. I'm an obscure writer whose novels never generated enough sales to warrant paperback editions. Rubbing the hump on the side of my third finger, misshapen by the red pencil I always hold too tightly, I quickly assume Guy has been commissioned by the Memphis Public Library system—that my portrait will hang in the new main library alongside the portrait of Shelby Foote, the most famous writer in

Memphis, famous all over the world for that matter. I shrink to fit the palm of Guy's hand.

Outside, the pallet of stones suddenly becomes a primitive square hut with a thatched roof and a splintered door.

I imagine a flock of pullets pecking the grass for bugs and a brown cow watching them. Our common ancestral name is Finn. For the heck of it I sometimes pronounce it with a French accent — *Fin*, like the end of something, but Guy and I are really of Irish descent, and much as I'd like to pretend otherwise, our common bond obliges me. I take off my cap and hook the hair behind my ears, wondering what I will wear.

***

I'm driving west on Poplar Avenue toward Guy's house. A storm gathers in the distance over the Mississippi River. Clouds drift like smoke, the atmosphere inside the Explorer airless and tropical. If my father were alive, he'd call it Banana Day.

The first time I heard him say it, I thought he meant a holiday set aside for going bananas, a day the mailman wouldn't come. I was then five-years-old and still snuggled in my bed, listening to the early morning sounds: my father's ritual raising of the bedroom window — already a few inches open for a good night's breath — to all the way up no matter what the prevailing weather conditions. My mother must have been listening too as she stole a few more moments of rest and planned her day. James wasn't born yet. As always, at the exact same moment John bumped in the side door from his paper route, my father said, "Out goes the bad air. In comes the good air." His perfect timing convinced me that John brought home the good air in his canvas sack. Growing up Catholic means thinking metaphorically at a very early age.

"Banana Day." My father closed the window with a bang, as if to postpone the celebration until he could participate. The bathroom door shut. From the shower he sang, "*Day-o. Day-a-a-ao.*"

I got out of bed, dressed quickly in yellow shorts and shirt, and outside on the front stoop waited for the neighbors to start acting as crazy as monkeys, the same as they did on the 4th of July, although some of them didn't need a holiday for an excuse. One for the money, two for the show, I waited to see them peel and eat whole stalks of bananas, to hear them whoop and shriek.

I nudged *The Commercial Appeal* toward the front door so that my father wouldn't have to be seen by the neighbors in his bathrobe when he opened the door to retrieve it. At the same time I wondered why John refused to bring our newspaper inside the house when he was the one who delivered it in the first place. It wasn't like it was out of his way or anything.

I felt my own impatience . . . the sweat rolling down my face in the morning heat, the fine wet hair on my arms. A cat bawled in the distance, the neighborhood otherwise silent. I'd begun to gnaw my fingernails when suddenly thunder cracked and it dawned on me that I was the only crazy monkey observing Banana Day.

More often than not I am still that same observer, waiting for something to happen.

The red light at Poplar and Parkway gives me time to watch the workers setting out a big municipal display of yellow marigolds on the median strip. Dogwoods and azaleas bloom under the canopy of oaks and yellow poplars, the old horse trail down the strip barely visible now in the new spring growth. Traffic moves forward. The golfers are out in Overton Park, a foursome of men carry their clubs across the old stone bridge.

Beyond them, deep in the old growth forest, the redbuds and native azaleas seem to be singing. Growing up, I thought of Mid-town Memphis as my playground. Everything in it still belongs to me. Somehow I've lived in each house, sitting on the porch swings, planting flowers in the window boxes, fixing the plumbing, mowing the lawns, re-screening the windows and doors, priming and painting.

Recently, Aunt Roux sold her house on Belleair Drive to Guy and moved to an apartment, but I still think of the house as hers, as if it bore the placard *House of Roux* along with the dates of her domicile.

I turn onto Belleair, a prized Memphis address, the grand houses in various architectural styles — Georgian, Tudor, Federalist, each one as proud as a church. Aunt Roux's low-slung, ranch-style house hugs the ground like a spread of crabgrass, an advantage when you live in the New Madrid Fault zone. A mild earthquake — about five on the Richter scale — would shake up houses all over town, cracking foundations, ceilings, and fireplaces, and I wonder why John and James, the *New Californians*, have traded one potential disaster for another. I hate thinking about the effects on Memphis if the Richter scale were to register at sixes and sevens. At least Aunt Roux's house wouldn't have far to fall.

The crumbling driveway widens in the back of the house where five old cars are parked, one of them on cinderblocks. A yellow-eyed yard dog tied to the bumper yaps and snarls, guarding the house as well as the two story garage — the lower level stuffed with old furniture and architectural salvage, above it Guy's studio with the Palladian window saved from a wrecking ball. The whole structure leans to the west, as if following the sun.

The dog strains his rope, his mouth foamy, so I back down the driveway and park the Explorer in the street.

Rain begins to fall, and I dart to Guy's front porch and ring the bell, shivering a little as I admire the exquisite moss growing on the pink stone. Aunt Roux and her late husband Charlton celebrated their fiftieth wedding anniversary in this house. Cousin Rosemary presented them with sweatshirts — 50 on the back, his blue, hers pink. Aunt Roux slipped hers on over her pale pink silk dress, mussing her hair a little, and continued to greet guests as if the sweatshirt were part of her ensemble.

The door opens to Guy's dreamy face, his bemused smile reminiscent of the portrait he painted of Elvis. I step inside the dark entry hall, sheets of hard-traveling rain blowing eastward as he closes the door behind me.

He looks me up and down disapprovingly.

My clothes are somewhat funereal and I imagine him at his easel, plunging my neckline and painting my gray outfit red.

He switches on the glaring ceiling light. I close my eyes for a moment, leaving my floaters in darkness. Protein deposits, the ophthalmologist calls them. Nothing to worry over. I think of them as tiny black fish swimming in my ocular ponds. I blink open, scattering the fish to Hell and back.

I brush the raindrops from my sleeves and look for things familiar, things that had belonged to our grandparents who died long before Guy and I were born, things likely moved to Aunt Roux's apartment now. Where the framed china plate painted with our Grandmother Maggie's face had hung, the lighter square appears as a window to a by-gone world . . . and I pause to remember her young face, her cascading red hair wild and free before marriage and childbirth cut and tamed it.

She was forty-five years old when our Grandfather Steve parked his car in front of the funeral home and shot himself. His photograph still hangs on the wall, as if Aunt Roux left the memory of her father behind for Guy to keep.

A big floor sander sits in the empty dining room, buckets of paint stacked in the corner, the whole place covered in sawdust.

Guy offers no comment about his project, and I follow his trail of footprints to the back of the house where the den door stands open to the rain-splashed patio. Another dog—this one black and white and looped to the clothesline, runs back and forth under the spreading oak tree and yaps at the gray cat positioned inside the door, just beyond the dog's reach.

Ping Pang. The leaking rain hits the buckets stacked under the skylight. Guy spaces them more strategically along the drip line, then he begins to clear the sofa of plunder. I set my purse and keys on the coffee table, and move a stack of magazines and a woolly scarf from an old leather chair. We both sit down.

The eight foot tall portrait of Elvis leans on the bookshelves. Apparently the Presley estate opted not to purchase it.

The Big Elvis electrifies the room and I imagine it hanging at Graceland and his fans flecking away the jewelled white suit with their fingernails in hopes of touching him naked. I still love *Mystery Train* and I sort of want to touch him myself.

In various stages of completion, other portraits are propped against the walls: a balding man with a mustache, a lady holding a birdcage, a baby dressed in a Christening gown. Each portrait seems to tell a story.

"Not in a hurry, are you?" He slumps into the old downy sofa and I begin to worry over the length of time the photo session might take. I wish I were back home carrying stones in the rain, feeling my wet clothes cling to my body. I let him know that I have other obligations. "Comb your hair."

He makes a show of struggling to his feet, then shuffles down the hall in search of his camera. I hear faint noises in the kitchen before the house again falls silent, and for a moment I wonder why Cecile and the kids don't come out and say hello to me. Cecile is Guy's third wife—two children with the first wife, two with the second, two more with Cecile, like pairs of shoes.

The water rises in the buckets and I haul them to the patio door two at a time, slosh them, then return for more. The black and white dog watches me from his doghouse.

The room becomes damp and a little steamy. Pushing up my long sleeves to just below the elbows, I sit down on the ottoman and worry over the effects of humidity on the paintings, especially Big Elvis who appears to be sweating.

At age thirteen, when I'd hear Elvis sing *I Was the One*, I was barely able to pull my ear away from the radio. John once took me to see him in concert—the Cotton Pickin' Jamboree they called it. In the crowded hallway of Ellis Auditorium, we saw Annie MacFarland, the girl John would ultimately marry and divorce. They nodded to each other without speaking. They had gone together, broken up, and now she was dating Elvis. She'd been seen on the back of his motorcycle at dusk. I didn't yet know how it feels to lose someone you love, but the dark circles under John's eyes told me that sleep didn't come easy now.

We sat in the first balcony and listened to the Jordanaires warm up the audience with their Gospel sound. The whole thing reminded me a little of our Protestant relatives on mother's side of the family hymn-singing around the piano — stanza after endless stanza — and I began to feel anxious.

When Scotty Moore, Bill Black and D.J. Fontana came onstage and started in playing, the crowd began to buzz, not steady like the insects you count on, but something erratic, volatile. Then Elvis bounded on stage in black pants, white shirt and Kelly green jacket, and the girls screamed their heads off! I was jumping inside, the blood about to burst from my veins, but I committed myself to silence, never made the first peep.

Beside me my brother sat in a blue funk. I hated seeing him that way. He'd been president of his high school class, captain of the football team, Elwood P. Dowd in *Harvey*. Elvis sang *Heartbreak Hotel* and *Long Tall Sally*, rolling his leg, swiveling his hips, making love to every girl in the place, and when he sang *I was the One*, my heart just about stopped. Still I kept silence, and in the flurry of flashbulbs, I pictured Elvis kissing Annie Mac, and John watching them.

Then Elvis sang *Hound Dog*, and the roaring crowd raised the roof! I sat on my hands, just kept counsel with myself, because I knew good and well that Elvis was nothin' but a *Wolf*.

Guy slides back into the room, camera in hand, and for the first time I notice his moccasins. I comb my hair with my fingers and ask about Cecile. "Fine," he says. He fails to ask about my spouse, so I volunteer that BD is also fine.

Driving rain pelts the earth, both dogs now barking in sync. The cat glides along the woodwork, stopping to claw the grass cloth wall covering. Guy doesn't seem to worry about the dogs or notice the cat; instead, he asks me about John and James.

I try to ignore the worrisome scratching noise. "John had a slight heart attack . . . he's okay . . . hikes all over California now. James started playing swing . . . listens to old Django Rheinhart records for inspiration."

Guy pats his chest and strums his fingers on his arm, carefully considering the news about his cousins. Stretching and purring, the cat sidles up to him and sits on his feet. Guy makes small talk about his own siblings—his brothers, Jim, B Roy, Ed, and his sister, Little Roux. Mostly, he seems to be listening and waiting for something. I'm thinking about my female cousins on both the Catholic and the Protestant sides of my family … the ones of us named after our mothers and grandmothers . . . Little Roux, Little Rosemary, Little Kate, Little June, Little Embie, Little Mawgrit, all of us still "Little" even though our namesakes — with the exception of Aunt Roux — are gone now.

When the doorbell rings, both dogs howl to heaven. "Scoot, Sam." Guy punts the cat that lands gracefully on the scatter rug, and I'm glad at least one of his pets has a name. Guy's up and in the entry hall, greeting someone in a muffled voice. He pauses at the den door, the visitor just behind him.

The two of them seem to have formed a line, and I adjust my glasses and wait several seconds before Guy finally stands aside and says, "Class reunion this weekend. Remember Matt?"

Suddenly, I'm on my feet gazing at green eyes the exact color of the marble I keep in my black box. I remember, oh how I remember Matthew Christopher Ames. *Ames to please, Ames high, Ames for the stars*!

"He was my sweetheart." The words slip from my lips and my heart flutters. He moved away from Memphis at age fifteen. No one else understood how it was with Matt and me. Behind his old bright eyes his young face smiles at me. He folds me in his arms, his dark rain-splattered shirt warm to the touch. His deep voice casts a net over time. "Now that I've found you, I don't think I can let you go."

We hold each other hard. I'm strong now—my hands, my arms—and I think I can hold onto him forever.

Tumbling through the skylight to the pots, the rain gives back the years—*plip plop diddley bop*, and I'm hearing a song I cannot peg for the life of me. The warmth spreads through my body, and I wonder if my short nails will buckle in the heat.

The cat circles our feet, and Guy tries to catch him. His voice comes out high-pitched and plenty worried.

"You're both married."

"We should be married to each other." Matt's words fog my glasses and I let go of him in the attempt to clear them. To look at him amazes me . . . still trim, athletic, not so handsome as to become tiresome, his sandy hair a little grayed at the temples, his expression still dark in a brood.

Guy says, "I'd forgotten you two were sweethearts. Coincidence you both show up at the same time."

I think he says this in case Aunt Roux finds out he conned me. He invites us to sit down, escorting me to one end of the couch, motioning Matt to the other end. He sits between us.

Matt and I run through the wheat fields of our

lives. After college and a stint at pro baseball, he served in the army in Laos. Later, he studied to become an architect.

I picture him seated on a stool at a drafting table, leaning forward on his elbows, pouring over the plans for a baseball stadium. Guy holds up his hand and asks about Laos. Matt looks at me and we both lower our eyes. Long ago we talked briefly about Laos and neither of us wants to talk about it again. Instead, we talk about our marriages, our children. I tell him about my work.

We talk through Guy as if he were a screen. He turns his head from one to the other, his attention wholly ours. I point to my throat, hoping he will offer us something to drink. He ignores my request with a hard frown that suggests he cannot trust us alone together in the same room.

"Talk about how you met," he insists.

Matt jumps right in. "I remember the first time I saw her. She was standing on the corner with a group of girls. She had on a blue sweater, a black skirt, and tan suede loafers. She wore black cat-eye glasses."

"I remember your plaid shirt and the jacket you wore. I remember your smile."

"Every time I'd call your house, James blasted me with 'EMMETT JAMES FINN speaking!' When you babysat him, we'd play Parcheesi. You'd think a six year old would get tired of Parcheesi. He never got tired of Parcheesi. I'd pick him up and threaten to bump his head on the ceiling if he didn't go to bed, and he'd have this big grin on his face, knowing damn well I wouldn't hurt a hair on his head and he was going to stay up as late as he damn well pleased. Then we'd try to wear him out playing chase or hide-and-go-seek."

Matt once called me Little Mama, but I don't say it. "Chase made him wild."

"It made us wild, too."

We are quiet for a moment, listening to jungle drums in the distance. The vein in my wrist pulses. The hair on my arms prickles, and then sadness changes the expression on his face, the flip side of a bright sun-filled day when the night comes down. I remember his exact same expression in a way that I remember nothing else.

He'd seem far away from me then, and I would imagine what all was inside his head — the nuts and bolts, threads and wires, the little hammers, gears, the cogs and the spinning wheels, and the heavy air would press down on me, doubt and fear overhead like a dark cloud, and silently I would hold his hand and wait for him to come back to me.

"I was ripped out of Memphis," he says from a deep black hole. His fists are stacked on his knee, his knuckles bony. I hear pages being ripped from a book—the middle and the end. Only the beginning survives.

Matt's father spoke to my mother. I heard only enough to know that the phone call was from him. Later that same day she spoke to me about the hard time Matt was having with the move. Maybe I could *talk to him*. They'd appointed me to be the strong one, only they couldn't see that I was standing on the edge beside him, looking down the same dark, winding slope.

Camera in hand, Guy stands up and snaps my picture. "Mawgrit, after I get the portrait started, you'll have to sit for me at least once."

He hands me the camera and I take a picture of the two classmates together. Matt takes one of Guy and me. Then Guy poses Matt and me—sort of a prom-photo we never had—and in the blinding flash I'm suddenly remembering Matt's profile in a baseball cap, the way I could easily pick him out of a cluster of teammates. I'm remembering him sliding into third base, his dust billowing my blue felt skirt as I stood watching from the sidelines. I remember the drapes patterned with big yellow tropical flowers and deep green foliage, the nubby green couch, the car lights on the window. I remember letting him out the back door at the exact same moment my parents came in the front. I remember his face against mine. I remember his hands on me. I tell them I must go.

Guy appears relieved and quickly ransacks the den closet for an umbrella, and failing to find one, he takes out a huge blank canvas instead.

Matt hugs me goodbye—the feel of him amazes me—then Guy breaks in to take my hand, quickly leads me out the front door and together we dart down the rutty driveway to the car, the rain peppering the canvas he holds above us.

As he opens the car door for me, he holds the canvas one-handed, a waiter with a big empty platter. His brown eyes are intense and purposeful. "Take it easy, girl." He shuts the door and walks across the lawn toward the house.

Matt's broad shoulders fill the doorway. He blows me a kiss. I blow it back to him. Overhead the thunder claps loudly. When the world came crashing down on Matt and me, the days wore hard edges, the space between us flat and endless.

I start the Explorer and turn on the radio. On WKLR Lightnin' Hopkins plays guitar. My heart thumps to his rhythm. The windshield wipers beat back and forth, in my eyes the school of fish swimming wildly. I head into the streets streaming rain and hold tight to the steering wheel to keep from sliding off the face of the earth. My mind travels back to the Parkway lined with old mansions, the route I'd travelled after he'd left town.

I was cooled by the moon, my old blue Schwin easy-rolling under the bowers of trees, my hair a streaming afterthought as I peddled under the trestle bridge and on past the Fairgrounds to the Parkway viaduct—calves straining toward the peak—then a rush of adrenaline back down again, taking the South Parkway curve effortlessly past the stately homes newly owned by Blacks.

People said nothing would be the same now — the grand houses likely to be painted chartreuse and fluorescent pink—but nothing had changed, excepting the black stone jockey holding a lantern at the entrance of a Greek Revival mansion, now absent from his post.

Rounding a curve, the terrain flattened out, my knees steadily pumping as the median narrowed and the Parkway suddenly slipped into decline. Under the canopy of trees, the streetlights were barely visible, leaving the small houses in darkness, the bushes alive with night sounds.

I hard-peddled past a cluster of black men on a corner drinking whisky.

A yard-dog barked and snarled from the porch of a rag-tag house where its red eyes glowed like hot coals.

In the shrubby of old Zion Cemetery, wispy black ghosts hovered over the wrecked tombstones. Somewhere above me was the moon I could no longer see. Passing a blues-blasting dive, the gutbucket sound of a soul scrubbed on a washboard shook my bones and set my stomach to rising. I gripped the handlebars and turned onto Matt's old

street, the sound of the blues still in my head. His father had told him they would be going on to a better life, raising the bar, a move for the good of the whole family. I knew Matt was gone, gone for good. Still, I had to see the empty house to know he wasn't there. Maybe some part of him was left behind: an old cap, a baseball, a pair of old tennis shoes.

I coasted to his old bungalow and slowed to a stop. Deserted, dark, flower pots gone from the porch, the sold sign in the yard--the permanence of fate glared back at me. The heaviness of air, the solid weight of it, slowed my breathing. I abandoned myself to the stillness. The night--the world itself-- stood vacant, as if no one had ever lived in it at all. I was alone now, would always be.

A rattletrap truck turned onto the street, the headlights suddenly on high beam exposing my white skin to the hot light, at once raising my consciousness and deepest fear out of some crevice. Only one way out of the cul de sac, I summoned all my strength and began peddling in the standing position, pressing my whole weight to the peddles, right then left, giving the truck a wide berth, averting my eyes as I passed it.

The truck turned around and followed me, shimmying so hard I expected its fenders, doors and hubcaps to fall off. At Parkway I peddled furiously to keep up with the traffic, my heart pounding up and over the viaduct--riders screaming from the Zippin Pippin and I thought it was myself screaming, until the sound got drowned in the hurdy-gurdy music of the Merry-Go-Round.

The median widened — I never looked back — my legs whirling all the long way back home where I arrived breathless and pouring sweat, my father peering at me and asking if I'd been playing the fainting game again ... the one where you'd take many deep breaths, then a friend would squeeze you around the middle until you passed out. Not a bad idea I was thinking. That way maybe I'd forget him--the loneliness abated, at least for a second or two. And now begins the search, all over again, for how I will live without him.

WAPANOCCA

The boy steered the little five-and-a-half-horse Johnson, unable to see over the head of the woman or past the broad shoulders of the man. They eased between the mud banks, the man silently pointing to logs that slept just under the green water.

Blue smoke poured from the motor, becoming iridescent in the sun streaks that appeared from spaces in the top bowers of white sycamores and old oaks.

The woman was much like an extra thumb on a wide hand. She did not look at the boy or at the man. Redwing tunes came like dots between the cries of the crows. The birds screamed as the boat crept through the narrow waterway that led to the lake.

Wapanocca was once part of the flood plain of the great Mississippi, but the river changed course, leaving the lake to feed on its own springs.

The boat, army green, nipped a log and ground down to a silence. The boy pulled up the motor. It had gathered a thatch of water vines. He unwrapped the prop and spun it.

"You look to know what you're doing," said the man.

The boy did not smile. He pulled the starter, elbow jerking back, holding onto the knob but letting the rope slack back into its house. The motor rested.

"Pull out the choke."

The boy obeyed. The motor spoke up, the boat rocking easily as the man shifted his weight.

The man opened a beer and swallowed gulps that bobbed his throat. "Go on across the lake. We'll try the water trail through the bogs."

The boat slid from the narrow passageway into the wide lake. The woman stared across the water looking for lily pads. She saw the man looking at her. "They haven't spread yet. It's too early." She said it with conviction, but she still looked for them.

She could see an angus on the other side of the lake in a flat clearing; an egret rode its head. The boat headed for the cypress trees, wide skirts rising from water to narrow waists craning upward like lean necks. Nesting houses for wood ducks stood on stilts in the cypress thicket. The boat snaked through the trees rapping on the knees that huddled near the big trunks like beggars. Turtles scuttered from log beds, disturbing the slime sheets growing on the water.

"Cut," said the man. "We'll troll."

He pulled up the trolling motor where it wouldn't run shallow.

"Shorten your cork."

The boy shook a cricket out of the screen holder and ran his hook into its sternum. He slid his float down close to his hook, then lowered it into a turtle hole in the slime. The woman copied the boy. She felt the warm bug and tried to place the hook into the thin outer skin.

"Do it quick," said the man. "You're stupid to sit there like some surgeon."

The man screwed up the side of his mouth, which made his cheek puff; his eye bulged slightly.

The woman's hand shook, the hook quivering in her jitters. She let the hook drop to the bottom of the boat, making a pinging sound. She put the cricket on an island of slime that was moving away as the boat stirred up the water.

"What in hell's name did you do that for?" The man threw his can overboard. It floated on the slime.

The boy rested his rod on the gunwale.

"I'll do you one."

She swallowed and allowed the boy to bait her hook. She watched as he quickly set her rod for use.

"You going to fish?" the boy asked him.

"I'm trolling. You can see that, can't you?"

He turned the boat into a space between the trees.

The boy tended his rod, moving, bobbing his hook, not letting a dragonfly rest on his line. Mud daubers sat on his knee. He let them stay.

The woman let her hook rest on the slime. She could pick it up and stay out of the trees that dripped over the boat. She did not want to get hung up on the limbs that reached for her rod as the boat skimmed past them.

Crows fought bluejays in the trees. The leaves were thickly set on the branches; the branches shook as the birds darted, flapping like fans.

She felt a drag. "Wait."

"You don't have anything. Don't you know when you're on bottom?"

She waved the rod first one way then the other trying to un-snag the line. The man careened about. He cut the motor and pulled water with his paddle. He reached his arm through the slime and pulled the hook from its catch of wood stems.

"Pay attention."

"You get hung up sometimes." The boy said this as he watched his own line.

"Don't get smart."

The man hacked at the water. Cold drops came into the boat. The water dots were green. The man opened a beer, but didn't drink it. He let it sit next to him.

"We'll try over near those cypress knees."

The woman hauled in her rod. The boy reached her hook and checked her bait.

"I'll do it next time," she said.

"No need."

"Shit."

The man had knocked over the beer, its warm foam spreading out on the seat down the fall line to the water. The man pitched the can over the side. He opened the ice box and got a new beer. He sat it beside him, pointed a finger at it.

The boat moved under the bird sounds almost in a grunt; the logs tried to catch the moving.

"You're going farther in?" said the boy.

"What are you?" glared the man. "Chicken shit or chicken salad?"

The boy did not answer. He looked at the woman, then reached for a cream soda.

"You're drinking too much of that stuff," said the man. "Makes your stomach soft and your teeth rot."

The boy put the soda back in the box.

"It's the first he's had," the woman said.

"You're making him into a chicken shit little girl," said the man. "You'd let him have anything he wants."

The woman looked up at the cypress branches, straining her neck, pulling the muscles in her throat taut, then settled into her shoulders, curving her spine into a slump. She crossed her ankles and stared into the trees. She knew the man was dying; she didn't know how to save him. The boy did not yet know about the dying.

The slim covered the water like a thick blanket. It was the same inside the man, the malignancy choking the life from his body and his dreams. The woman looked back.

She saw the path where the boat had been, the slime slowly moving over it. The motor whirred, refusing to turn. The man pulled it up and shortened its stride.

"Too shallow?" asked the boy.

"Maybe."

The boat scraped a log and bucked it.

"Shit."

The man rocked back and forth trying to ease the boat off the log. "Shift your weight, both of you."

The woman watched his movements and leaned back and forth as he moved. He did the same. The boat stubbornly sat on the log refusing to give up its resting place.

The man held the side of the boat and slipped into the water.

The woman looked for snakes.

"What does it feel like?" asked the boy.

It feels like slime shit. What did you think it'd "feel like?" He rocked back and forth, bouncing it, sliding it, rubbing the bottom against the log with a screeching sound sure to scrape a sore on the metal. The boat came free.

The man pulled it well clear of the log.

"Call on a man to do a man's work." He got in the boat with slime clinging to his knees, wrapping his calves, growing down into his shoes.

"I'll scull."

He found the paddle and dipped its splintered edge in the slime, flattening the slender part to his skin where it became a part of his arm twisting with the motion of his wrist.

He eased the boat toward the knees, waffling the paddle, zig-zagging in and out of the trees, sculling, moving forward.

"It's cool enough. We'll catch some crappie back here if they haven't all choked to death on this green shit."

He picked the algae off his gray pants, then wiped his hands on his seat.

The woman cast into the water; the dead cricket hit a cypress bow, and her line straightened with the movement of the boat.

"Wait."

"Why in hell's name would you cast? Just drop the damn thing in the water near the trunks."

He took her rod and pulled toward the tree. He took a knife from his tackle box. He cut the branch and freed her line.

"You don't have to be plain stupid."

The boy moved his float and watched it bob.

The woman laid down her rod. "I don't think I'll fish anymore."

"Don't sulk. You'll likely have him doing the same thing by and by."

"Tell him, then," said the woman quietly. "It's why we came. It was you who said he should begin to accept what's to come."

"There's time enough," he said. "I have my way of doing things."

The boy looked hard at his float, a red-orange harvest moon in the water. His float hardly moved in the thick green growth. She saw him yawn and begin to look about.

"Look there." He pointed to the water's edge where they were headed. A big raccoon held on to the side of an oak high above the ground.

The man had been watching the coon for several minutes. The woman had seen the man's eyes, blue like turquoise glass, pensive in a brood, watching the target, thinking, talking inside to some spirit that she did not know.

"What are you thinking?" she asked.

He ignored her and kept looking at the coon.

"He must be restless," said the man. "Usually do their scavenging at night."

The coon stayed quiet, not moving, like a growth on the tree, his muzzle masked like a thief, his ringtail growing straight down like an aged blackened vine.

"Can't catch a fish. You can get yourself a coon instead."

The boy smiled and quietly put down his rod. The man opened his silvery tackle box dented from years of use and took a twenty-two pistol, its snout pointing like a black finger, from the bottom. It had been hidden under the shelf of jigs beside the scaling knife sheathed in its rawhide scabbard like a bandage.

"You load it yourself."

He handed the boy six shells and then gave him the gun. The boy opened the gun and held the barrel to the light, checking it. He spun the barrel, then loaded it.

The man eased the boat to the shore.

"Isn't it out of season to kill a coon?" the woman asked.

"You have to do with what comes," said the man.

The boy steadied his arm with his left hand, closed his left eye, and aimed at the coon. He held his breath; his finger, curved on the trigger, pulled to send the crackling through the air, the sound echoing back as the animal fell, scraping its claws on the scab bark. It hit the ground, a thud sound on the mud--and screamed. The woman felt it was herself screaming. The boy's mouth stood open, his face a sick yellow.

"Put him out of his misery," ordered the man.

The woman's chest filled with the coon hollers. She could hear the clattering of her bones as she reached out to touch the hand of the man. His eyes, now deep in their sockets, gazed out at her. He allowed her hand to remain on his skin while the gun gave off a second crack.

She lifted her hand, then held her own arms. She turned back to look at the boy. His face was furrowed as he unloaded the gun. He was calm, but she knew that he was not safe now, would never be.

Cane Brake

Most likely Bud's bilirubin caused him to hit Pete over the head with the flashlight. Bud's portals block the confluence of his waters. Annie Peeper imagines a salmon as it tries to swim up streambeds that are shrinking. She wonders if the liver transplant will sweeten up Bud's disposition.

In the cafeteria her nineteen-year-old son Pete sits across from her at the table and eats fried chicken and mashed potatoes smothered in cheese.

Near them medical personnel, hospital workers, and relatives of patients eat with rare dedication, their plates piled with potatoes, black-eyed peas, meat loaf, macaroni, and slices of coconut pie, as if hearty food insures their own immortality.

If immortality were an elective, Annie would choose something else instead — a few years of perfect seasons, or a friend who understands you even when you express yourself badly.

Pete's hair curls handsomely around his ears, his face puffy from lack of sleep, his eyes nonetheless a clear sky blue. He wears one of Bud's old plaid flannel shirts, his first time ever to accept one of his father's hand-me-downs.

"The insurance company's going bust on this one," he says, lolling his tongue to cool the hot cheese. "They can't keep footing the bill for the big ones unless they raise the premiums so high people can't pay."

"They always pay. People are more scared of bankruptcy than death."

She looks at his plate, little sand dunes of white food. Annie never could get Pete interested in nutrition. On his forehead the odd little smart knot near the cove of his hairline never fails to remind her of the flashlight.

Pete loads white beans on his fork and into his mouth. He removes a sliver of green pepper from his tongue.

"He's lucky to get a new liver after what he did to the old one. It's like setting fire to your own house and then collecting."

Lately worry over the solvency of the insurance industry has taken hold of him, his moral stand defined, and she wonders when he began listing to the political right. She didn't notice when. Not long ago he was consumed with sympathy for the homeless and the downtrodden, blaming their plight on big business. She looks at the food on her plate and doesn't remember choosing it. Certainly not the crimson Jello. The cafeteria buzzes with voices and it's easier not to talk.

Pete attends college now and she assumes he drinks beer and maybe liquor. She wonders if he knows when to quit, if he's ever gotten drunk. She worries that someday he'll follow in his father's footsteps and be on the receiving end of a transplant. She shudders in the cold cafeteria. Her own family as well as Bud's is rife with alcoholics, most of them dead now. She spears a lettuce leaf, tries to focus on the bright green color, but slips instead to the snowy regions of her mind where the volatile years of domestic life stand as an impregnable Ice Age, a force that slides over you and slowly carves hills, valleys, plateaus, has its way with you until you bear its imprint. She imagines empty bottles of vodka standing as tombstones in a frozen cemetery.

"You okay?" Pete's eyes shine like glass over the rim of his tumbler of ice tea. On top of his head his dark brown hair is slicked back thirties-style. The curly sides seem ill at ease.

She shakes her head and quickly gulps her tea, purging her mind of bad thoughts. The sun leans westward toward the Mississippi River leaving the courtyard outside in shadow. Behind Pete, the dwarf magnolia looks black against the plate glass window.

Crazy to allow the years to set in and harden you.

Waiting with Bud for the call, she'd slept poorly of late, her will power flimsy, her own electrolytes going haywire.

Pete swallows a large bite of chicken. "I oiled all of his guns before I came down here."

"He'll appreciate that," she says, knowing full well that Bud would probably say the guns didn't need oiling, that Pete wasted his time.

When Bud became too ill to drive to the bottomland where he'd hunt, he began shooting squirrels in the backyard, loading his rife with c.b.'s––special 22 bullets that gave off only a ping sound. He'd skinned and dressed out the squirrels, and froze them in plastic bags up to the time when his hands began to cramp so bad he could no longer hold a knife. Then he started to feed the squirrels instead of shooting them.

Pete holds the chicken leg as a club and glances at his multifaceted watch that gives the time in countries as far away as Australia.

"He's been under the knife for exactly seven hours and fifteen minutes now."

"Mickey Mantle's took ten, didn't it?"

"Longer, I think," says Pete. "Sixteen for Hagman."

"*Dallas* never seemed real. I never watched a whole show."

121

They both know full well about the hugeness of the operation and its expected length of time, a thing they've calculated at least twice within each passing hour. She remembers the bile-spewing character Hagman played and finds it difficult to empathize. On the other hand, Mickey, the worn-out hero, hangs out in the lighted corner of her consciousness, smacking a home run. In the end, Mantle's estranged family made up with him.

She piddles with her salad, scooting the ring of green pepper to the middle. She remembers trout fishing with Bud and the boys in the Ozarks. The White River flows through Arkansas crisp and cold as a revelation. Everything seemed clear to her then. The trout hide under flat rocks, their glinty frozen shadows suddenly disappearing the same as time and circumstance. Sycamore trees grow in low water near the river's edge, their roots exposed like family secrets.

Annie wonders how shallow roots sustain such large trees. In early spring, before the sycamores leaf, parasitic clumps of green mistletoe dot the top branches. Great Blue Herons nest in the mistletoe, staying with their young until the summer heat sends morning fog over the river, signalling the time for flight.

Their oldest two sons accepted jobs in other cities.

cities. She suspects sometime soon Pete will go far away. She envies the space out front of him, where he will go and what he'll see when he gets there, what she might have done if Bud hadn't gotten sick. She shrugs it off. Never would she give away her rusty Schwin with two flat tires, nor would she pump them up. Never would she give away her dead mother's hats—the florals, bowlers, or the pill boxes—nor would she wear them. Never would she sell her AT&T, not even at an all-time high.

"What time is it in Australia?"

She hears her voice dip to fill the spaces of silence. Pete turns his wrist so she can see his watch. Trays and silverware clatter in the crowded cafeteria, enough noise to waylay an appetite, but he eats determinedly.

She marvels at how her three sons have treated their father's illness. Telephone calls once a week. Occasional letters. How narrow is the chasm between dispassion and heartlessness?

Pete starts in eating the rice he's saved for last. "What will he be like when it's over? His old rebel self?"

"You know they don't transplant unless you've reformed." She moves the salad plate across the table as if to serve him her iceberg lettuce. Something inside her rises whenever she defends Bud.

She hopes drugs improve his disposition. If Bud becomes more docile, Pete might lighten up. George and Joe might come home more often.

She wonders how it might have been if George or Joe or Pete had squared off and hit Bud just one time — knocked him to the ground, bloodied his nose. Would he have stopped drinking?

Just last week she taught her high school history class that one big battle often serves as a turning point toward peace. The big father-son fight she managed to hold-off, now stands as the unresolved thing she most regrets.

"If he makes it home, I'll stick around and help you for a while. After that, I'm gone."

"You're still mad about the flashlight."

While Bud's liver was eating itself up, he paced, cussed and took medicine to stay alive. Several times his ammonia level shot up and he became disoriented, refusing to go to the hospital, and in a collaborative effort, firemen, policemen, and ambulance drivers coming to their assistance.

Neighbors gathered to watch the sideshow. When Bud's bilirubin shot the moon, he found the strength to whack Pete over the head with the flashlight, blood streaming down his face.

She remembers Bud thunking his sons on the head when they'd fail to properly skin a squirrel, scale a fish, or pluck a duck. Or cut the grass short enough. Bud would tump over a bucket and sit down on it, whittling a stick while they carefully waxed his truck until it mirrored their faces . . . and Bud's when he came from behind to inspect it. The sons, she admits to herself, *are* independent––three independent cusses, as Bud would say, and all three of them now seem proud to be included in his assessment. They'd passed some test beyond the realm of her understanding. Somehow Bud had preserved his sons the same as the hides he'd tanned.

"I want him to hike the Appalachian Trail with me," says Annie. "From Maine to Georgia. I've always dreamed about following the same path as the pioneers. I want to stand on top of a mountain and see where I'm going, and where I've been." To say such things out loud surprises her.

"He'll show you how to read a map and he'll answer all your questions about the forests, but he's not about to follow any trail." Pete looks Annie directly in the eyes and puts his fork down on the plate. "And he won't answer questions about anything else . . . such as why he wouldn't stop drinking until it came down to all this."

Annie sighs. Ask Bud a question about alcohol or his illness and he'd snap like a turtle, even when the questions came from doctors at the transplant clinic.

A doctor would bustle into the examining room, flurried and impatient, and see one hundred and forty pounds of Bud, wearing the navy blue wool shirt that kept him from freezing in summer, sitting ill and shrunken on the table with his thin arms and legs dangling as he popped his suspenders that held up his jeans, his little pouch of stomach as distended as a refugee's. He'd howl a greeting in the old irascible voice of a river man trudging from the bottoms.

"Old Doc," he'd say, though not one of the doctors was more than forty-five or so.

Invariably the doctors would stare wide-eyed as if face to face with an anachronism, A Southern Sasquatch, a Booger from the bottoms. Bud ignored his illness and told stories about fishing the old oxbow lakes of the Mississippi River or shooting white tail deer with a muzzle loader. The vitality in Bud's voice lied about his own condition.

Bud filled the freezer with game and fish, mostly venison, ducks, dove and crappie, but occasionally raccoon and possum.

"Deer hunting in Tennessee's just a harvest, Doc," he'd say. "More deer than you can shake a stick at." He'd tell the doctors about the meals she cooked. "Guess what was under the carrots and potatoes last night?"

Bud brought the doctors packages of frozen fish

and game, his generosity suspect since he no longer owned the enzymes to digest protein.

Outside in the courtyard, a slight wind dapples the shadows of the specimen trees, and Annie watches the intricate pattern of crepe myrtle wispy on her plate. Bud might have some Native American blood in him, Chickasaw or maybe Cherokee. Never can you hear his footsteps. Even in the dry leaves of fall, Bud remains illusive.

A nurse comes to the table. She wears a practiced smile. "Dr. Ramirez wants you to know everything's going well. It'll be some time yet. We'll keep you posted."

Pete gives her thumbs up sign.

Annie eats a bite of Jello, the sweetness an unwelcome taste, and wishes she didn't have to swallow. Over the past months — illness stretches time so that she could no longer remember exactly how long — she would accompany Bud to the clinic.

The waiting room was filled with sick people needing new livers, lungs, pancreases, and kidneys. She tried to guess what organ each one needed. She easily picked out Bud's competition. Except for the black people whose jaundice was hidden--the liver patients looked the yellow of a banana in various stages of ripeness. Bud referred to the liver people, including himself, as "yellow-eyed yard dogs."

Under the fluorescent lights of the examining room, his jaundice seemed an otherworldly fugue.

The transplant surgeons, now performing the huge operation, emmigrated from South America — Venezuela, Chili, Brazil — each one swarthy, handsome and boiling blood of the ancient Spanish, and sexy to Annie's way of thinking. She reminded Bud not to say the word "Spic."

The surgeons remind Annie of bullfighters — transplantation the biggest, most exciting operation commonly executed. You can see in their posture, *perfecto*, and in their quick dark eyes, a lust for drama and triumph.

"Mom, you ought to eat something."

She isn't afraid of somebody else's death — least of all Bud's — but still it seems inappropriate to eat. Dr. Esteban Ramirez flew to the donor site and harvested the liver. Then he inspected the organ to make sure it could serve a second time. Annie tries to suppress her feeling about the ghoulish process.

If it all works out, a dead stranger will take part in Bud's life. She wonders if the spirit of the dead stranger comes along in the bargain. "What if he gets a woman's liver?"

"What if he gets the liver of a black person? Or a Mexican? Maybe he'll speak with a different accent. Might be an improvement."

Pete's shirt criss-crosses over his chest like a series of railroad tracks. Maybe the liver belongs to a man just starting out in life — the young man dies, his liver lives, Bud becomes guardian. *He better damn well take good care of it.*

She looks at her son and tears flood her eyes. She quickly blots them with her napkin, then puts it back in her lap.

"You look tuckered," says Pete, using Bud's expression, and they both laugh.

Suddenly George and Joe are standing there. They buy coffee, they sit down. The questions come, first one, then the other. They want to know everything. How he looked when the call came, what he said. Pete tells them and she listens, nodding, rocking back and forth on her elbows. They look like Pete, only older.

She's worn the same long brown cotton dress for twenty hours and looks frumpy in the window's reflection. She'd put on the dress to visit Memphis Brooks Museum of Art where she'd been for an hour with the cellular telephone in her purse, feeling the weight of it pull on her shoulder as she viewed the works of Carroll Cloar. *Where the Southern Crosses the Yellow Dog,* she was looking at that when the ring startled her and she fumbled in her purse for the phone.

"Come on home now, Annie," he said. "I gotta be going on down there."

On the way home, careful not to speed and get stopped for a ticket, she met every red light on Poplar Avenue.

When she'd pulled in the driveway, Bud stood limply looking at the sky and trees, blowing his crow call in short bursts, a crow cawing back to him.

Slowly he got himself into the car and looked her in the eyes, almost smiled, then glanced down at his arms and legs and feet, his wasted body. He hung the crow call on the rearview mirror, then slipped inside himself and said nothing.

"He'll take a lot of medicine," she tells them. "Cyclosporine for the rest of his life and a lot of other drugs. Maybe nineteen or twenty different kinds."

"He'll cuss every pill he swallows," says Pete.

George and Joe laugh knowingly.

"They say the body never forgets," she says. "Rejection you live with."

A few years back when Annie was walking with Bud in the deep woods of the Mississippi Delta, she stopped and dug an ostrich fern with her small folding camp shovel, slipping the blade along the drip line, then deeper, loosening the roots, so intent on the work she forgot she wasn't the only person in the world.

She disturbed the leaf mod and smelled the dark humus. She dug clumps of wood fern and maidenhair and May apple, taking only one of each, working slowly as the green world enfolded her in leaves, an almost nitrogen narcosis that blurred her vision and set time adrift. The sky filtered through the leaves and from above she'd felt the endless protection of a lace net. The cry of a blue jay awakened her to the reality — that she couldn't pick up and carry the other plants — by herself. Then she looked around for Bud.

Through the trees she saw black squirrels and redwings. A white tailed deer skirted the top of a ravine. She squinted and focused, but she never saw Bud. She turned around in place, looking hard in a circle as she went, and still no Bud.

Not daring to step outside the circumference, she turned faster until her head spun, whirling within the compass of her vision. She sat down hard on the ground to quell the dizziness. She closed and opened her eyes, feeling the veins in her temples near to bursting.

Not more than five feet away Bud leaned against a tree, his body shaped by the slope of its form, his arm grown straightaway from the trunk as a branch would grow.

Then he moved slightly, shifting his shape, and

again she'd lost sight of him. And she'd known for a moment, while she sat perfectly still on the ground, that if this were the last day on earth, she'd want very much to spend it with Bud.

Inside the iridescent browse of the cane brakes she spots his new liver hanging from a branch like a hornets' nest, and she waits for him to reveal himself in the beating of an insect's wings, hears his breath, his voice in the caw of a crow, and in the hollow of her old wooden heart, she feels a rush of his wild green air.

House of Fury

The day Little Walter Jacobs got killed in a fight, John Ed teared up and grieved over him—a black musician he'd never even met—and wished upon a star. Not a squeak, nor a squall of harp, came from his room for three days.

She leaned her ear to his door, John Ed in there jawing with Otis Mabon.

"Rene Fury, you ought to be ashamed of your nosey self," she muttered, straining to catch every word. Fish or cut bait she'd committed to raising John Ed and ignorance wasn't nobody's bliss. Blame what deserved blame . . . a grandboy so full of blues he couldn't think straight. All that music set John Ed on edge. If he ran off with a Negro band, it wouldn't surprise her none. Bad as he played, they'd take him in anyhow . . . make his tote their drums and guitars. They'd like nothing better than to make a slave out of a white boy.

John Ed on edge, she likened the sound of it to a sharp knife before getting back to her job, which was eavesdropper, or spy. She took pride in her ability not to get caught at it, but hard as she listened — ear to his door — she got nothing but blues-talk, stuff about the life and times of Little Walter ...him playin' Willie Dixon's hoochie coochie songs, workin' with Big Bill Broonzy and Muddy Waters, eatin' chili at Sunbeam Mitchell's.

"Some old joint," she grumbled aloud to herself. "Just like a black man to call hisself Sunbeam."

The door opened. Quickly she straightened herself. Otis said, "Hi Miz Fury. Thought I heard somebody."

"Otis, can't you get him to stop playing for a few minutes? Give a body a rest?"

"Ain't likely he'd take my advice on that one, Miz Fury. He's what you might call hot-wired. Problem is, he got a short somewhere."

A daddy longlegs crawled on the ceiling and for a moment she wondered how it might feel up there walking across the sky, looking down on the world. She squashed the spider with the head of the dust mop, leaving a blood smear on the paint.

"You got that one, Miz Fury. Got him good." Otis stepped back into John Ed's room and shut the door.

Rut wouldn't like the smearing one bit. He'd want her to flick the daddy longlegs to the floor with the mop, then stomp it politely. Hard set notions, Rut was aptly named.

John Ed started in playing harp. Pity poor Otis in there so close and having to pretend he was listening to something better than noise. She stuck her fingers in her ears and wiggled them.

John Ed could hit a sour note and hold it longer than the City of New Orleans when it rumbled and screeched through town. He'd listen to a Little Walter record, then try and copy it.

Trouble was he never listened hard enough. For weeks she'd heard *My Babe* pumping out of the record player — so often she thought she could play the song herself — but John Ed wasn't likely to get it down no matter if he played it till judgment day, pity the thought.

Listen. Listen to your own heartbeat, she wanted to tell him.

Otis started in playing guitar and kept the beat — *somebody* had to — and as she pushed the dust mop side-to-side down the hall toward the front door, erasing herds of footprints, she wished with all her heart for a miracle. If God truly lived in each one of us like they say, why wouldn't he tune up John Ed? It was enough to make you lose religion if you had it in the first place.

The house was by far the best she'd lived in. The path from front door to back never failed to remind her of how far she'd come from the old shotgun house down in Mississippi, and need more be said? She'd left there to get away from the blues and how she'd ended up living them every day of her life was beyond all. Mop, scrub, dust, for the life of her she just couldn't get rid of the blues.

The hall divided the house in half — parlor, dining room and kitchen on one side, Rut's and her bedroom, the bathroom and John Ed's room on the other. The Uncles — what Rut called their four grown sons once John Ed came to live in the house — were spread out in one big room upstairs. And how in the world had that all happened? All of them back home to stay. She figured she'd done something bad wrong to deserve it.

She worked toward the back door past the pictures hanging on the wall — the Uncles in short pants and brown leather high-tops back when their shoes were little enough to spit shine, several shots of them bigger in their baseball suits and caps holding mitts and bats, and one of baby John Ed naked as a jay with his little butt stuck up in the air, his tiny hands clutching a terry beach towel with a biplane printed on it, altogether out of control and holding on for dear life. He cried then as loud as he played now. She wanted to fly off on her dust mop and escape his music, easy enough when the roof lifted off the house, which might happen any second now.

He wasn't mindful of the tune and she figured Otis couldn't stand it much longer. She resented Otis, but not without pity.

Sure enough, holding his ears he opened the door and nodded toward her with a knowing look, like they had something in common, which was putting up with John Ed. She'd heard of black saints. Maybe Otis was one of them. Besides guitar, he played several other instruments, two at a time if he felt like it. He wore his harp on a chain. If his neck turned green, you'd never know it.

He said, "Furious John Ed gargled the whole way through that one."

She straightened the framed embroidery of lilies-of-the-valley and roses hanging on the wall and pretended she hadn't heard Otis. He was right, of course. John Ed played so hard you'd think he was mad at the world, his face red and every note choked with his saliva.

She wished she had a nickel for every Marine Band harmonica she'd bought for John Ed. He'd started off with A and steady as you please lightened her pocketbook to G, each new harp sounding no better than the one before. She'd developed an ear, could tell a C harp from an A, a B-flat from an E. Mostly he played Cs, and she'd bought a bunch of them. Stop spittin' into his harps, they wouldn't rust on him.

Otis buffed his fingernails on his jeans. You had to give Otis credit for pride. Not reason enough to associate with him, but John Ed would do well to take care of himself that same way. The word for Otis was fastidious, though she'd never say it above a whisper for fear somebody'd think she'd up and rose above herself. She was born plain and no reason to pretend otherwise. That didn't keep her from fooling around with the words in her head — mix, match, sometimes fit them together like pieces on a quilt.

Otis leaned on the doorframe. He shut his big eyes and started in snoring. In truth, she didn't understand how he'd lasted in there so long without a break. She marveled how a Negro could sleep on his feet just like a horse. Her son Mel Ray could do that same thing and sometimes she wondered if maybe Rut's side of the family had a little drop of black blood from way back.

She was positive it hadn't come from her own mingy Church of Christ people, not one of them lively enough to keep up with a Negro. She'd long ago quit the Church of Christ.

Chin to chest, Otis was snoring softly. Back when he and John Ed were both twelve years old and met up for the first time at the Boy's Club in the old Fire Station, Otis had seemed smarter than a black boy had a right to be. They'd learned to tie every knot you'd ever heard of. She remembered how hard they'd worked with each other, tying and untying the slipknot, square knot, half hitch, and the sheep shank, and how plain tickled they'd be when they'd get one right, nine out of ten times Otis the first to get it. She figured neither one would ever work on a farm or boat and saw the knots as useless, the same as the two of them playing music together. She'd warned Rut about John Ed getting tied up with Otis.

"Them boys is okay," was all he'd say.

Give Rut enough rope and he'd hang hisself along with the rest of the family. Ask for trouble and it'll find you every time. John Ed and Otis were both fifteen now — the two of them together an accident just waiting to happen or a big bomb about to explode. Raising a crowd of boys himself, had Rut leaned nothing?

Otis stirred and kept on snoring. After putting up with John Ed, he deserved his rest. She slipped quietly toward the back door a few feet away and opened it, feeling the cold airflow through the screen.

She breathed in and out, calming her frayed nerves. Too bad the screen couldn't sieve some of the louder notes, if only for the neighbors' sake. She'd promised to take care of John Ed, but had just about run out of steam.

On the other hand, old Londeen was half deaf and not one bit perturbed by it. Lucky Londeen couldn't hear thunder.

A crow screamed across the sky and then perched on a high branch of the sycamore tree in the drizzle. Back when Rene was a girl readying herself for school on a cold, rainy day, her mama would warn of quinsy.

"Bundle up," she'd say.

Rene remembered the old red wool stocking cap topped with a snowball, unraveling year by year until only the ball was left. Her mama bobby-pinned it to her hair anyhow.

The crow flew from the tree and swooped to a telephone pole sunk in the backyard, most likely looking for road-kill or garbage. Didn't have to look far. Garbage had started piling up back in January after some of the men stayed off the job.

Here it was March—alive with stink—and nothing settled yet. They'd likely remember this one as the year Memphis smelled like a cesspool.

Old crow couldn't sit still, likely because of the noise. She wished John Ed would take up another instrument, but he had small hands, probably too small for anything much bigger than a harp. He got mad when she suggested a ukulele.

The crow flicked its wings and flew down to the clothesline near John Ed's window and perched there, slicking its feathers. The back wall cut in at John Ed's room, a square piece cut from a square cake. Rene figured the original owners got cheated by the builder. The angle from the back door allowed her to see into John Ed's windows if she craned her neck and narrowed her eyes to a bead.

Otis startled her from behind.

"Make some noise, Otis," she said. "Don't' just sneak up behind somebody. You part Indian or something?"

"Blackfoot," he smiled, and she held up her hand to block the glare of his blinding white teeth. Nothin' you could say offended him.

Just then John Ed played a note high as the shrill whistle at the snuff factory, scaring away the crow and quivering her nerves. She and Otis both stoppered their ears with their fingers.

"Hold on," said Otis. "He got to come for air sometime."

A grandmother doesn't take well to criticism of her grandboy, not even if what Otis'd said was the truth plain and simple. Nonetheless, her ears rang and she committed to buying earplugs for both of them. Hard enough Otis being a Negro without him going deaf on top of it.

Several crows landed on the garage and cawed their heads off. She'd always known crows could talk, and she wished to understand what they said — maybe secrets of the world not in the Bible. "They know things," she said, holding herself quite still.

"I know that's true," said Otis.

He seemed certain.

She cracked her knuckles and rubbed the arthritic protrusions at the base of her thumbs. Otis's face was the color of coffee with cream. His big farsighted eyes, black and full of fire, were magnified by the glasses.

"You're getting wet, Otis. You'll likely take cold."

"You hear the sanitation workers down the street? Rain or shine, they keep at it. Rain ain't going to melt me. You the one liable to take sick. End up in a puddle."

She ignored Otis. Feel sorry for the downtrodden and the have-nots means you feel sorry for yourself, and that's the last thing in the world she needed. And when had *garbage* got changed to *sanitation*? Who was in charge?

"You ought to go on home now, Otis."

Still in her head were the two men killed in a garbage truck back in February.

Without a word Otis went back into the house to gather his belongings. The screen slapped behind him.

Rene's mind crawled through briars and honeysuckle thickets to what she hated remembering back when she was a girl. She'd seen a black man

142

named Willie Lum hanging from a tree, a thing that had turned her inside out. His eyes had popped out of his head and plunked on the ground like sweet gum balls, picking up moss and sticks, rolling fast toward the bush where she was hidden.

She'd jumped up and run the whole way home with her heart pounding out of her chest. She scrambled up the porch steps and held so tight to the splintered post the palms of her hands got stripped of skin.

Never did she speak one word of what she knew. Her throat felt parched, so dry she could hardly swallow. She'd known Willie Lum. Make friends with one of them and you find yourself holding a sack of something you got no use for. She wished Willie Lum had never been born.

The screen of John Ed's window opened and thin-as-a-reed Otis dropped to the ground, managing not to bust the branches of her leafless hydrangeas. Hollow boned like a bird, she thought.

Otis, we got doors. No sense you coming and going through the window. Somebody looking would think you were up to no good."

"Just practicing. Can't go to jail for practice."

In his orange poncho he looked like an umbrella at half-mast. Careful not to bang it, John Ed slid the guitar out the window to Otis's long spidery fingers and he slipped it under the poncho and over his shoulder. It stuck out front of him like a shotgun. Londeen would be watching. She hated that about old lady Londeen — Queen behind the Screen, Mel Ray called her. Always peering.

"Good-bye, Otis," she said, anxious for him to get gone.

"You won't be seeing me tomorrow, Miz Fury," as if she'd counted on him, as if she'd cry bitter tears if he didn't show up. He didn't budge, just stood waiting for her to look at him so he'd get in the last word.

Bad as she tried not to, she felt her neck turning toward him, creaking as it went, her whole body needing a good oiling.

He said, "Dr. King's coming to town."

She guessed the poncho wasn't all that warm. In it Otis looked like a giant tropical bird. She studied him rolling and rippling down the driveway. Orange, the color of madness.

He slapped his thigh with one hand, held his harp to his mouth with the other, and got off a screech as high and loud as the work whistle at the snuff factory. Garbage drums and cans were lined along the median strip beside the sidewalk on Mabel Avenue, and he kicked each one in passing.

2

"Boy howdy, we're having a big good one tonight!"

The words trudged out of Rene's throat like heavy feet up from the basement. In the kitchen she started in fixing the cornbread.

"Two cups of flour, " she sang out to no one in particular. "One cup of corn meal. One-fourth teaspoon of paprika."

When the words got out in the open air, she doubted the results and started adjusting proportions and substituting ingredients.

She sniffed at the cabbage and turnip greens boiling in two big iron pots on the stove, knowing full well Rut and the Uncles, John Ed too, wished she'd serve one or the other and not both, but her interest in cooking centered on volume more than on correlative taste, something they'd never understand and she wasn't about to waste her breath trying to explain it. Rut said she kept the family around her just for an excuse to cook big.

Little Walter's harp came full blast from John Ed's room. She was grateful it wasn't John Ed himself starting up. Still, she wished for pure silence. She enjoyed the kitchen noises she made and her own thoughts as they ran through her head — smells kin to her own mama's kitchen, the plump dumplings, brown biscuits, and vegetables grown and cooked just so by her mama's hands, the only part of long ago she cared to remember.

She looked at her own hands, the brown spots like cow ponds, murky and shallow between the swollen blue-river veins. The pots hissed and gurgled and sang. She left the past behind, and through the rising steam glimpsed the future … John Ed, sporting a dilapidated hat and a goatee and wearing a shiny black silk shirt, playing harp in a band with Otis and a bunch of unidentified Negroes. He'd never eat a proper meal.

She dabbed at her sweaty forehead with the hem of her apron. The serious business of getting the meal out kept her rooted in the present where John Ed was safe in his room eating Cheetos and spoiling his supper.

Mean Old World came from his record player, warbling in her head, and she hummed along because she could not stop herself—could not stop herself because she heard John Ed creeping up the stairs to the Uncles room and she knew what he was doing and what she'd have to do because of it!

Replace what he pilfered, that's what she'd have to do. Already she'd spent a wad of money on him.

Soon the warm spring days would cause Rut and

the Uncles to stay gone hours more, painting until "dark-thirty" as Joe would say first, then Franko would repeat over and over again ... a "dark-thirty" that would add dollars to their pay and more hours for John Ed to steal it. To afford his thievery she'd have to cut back on provisions. The idea of it made her woozy and set her stomach to fluttering.

Overhead the floorboards creaked. She opened her drawer filled with coupons clipped and never used, coupons that cut the cost of packaged food she didn't hold with eating in the first place — probably stale if the truth were known.

To use coupons would mean changing her way of cooking! With a loud bang she shut the drawer on any such possibility. Why had she saved them in the first place?

She'd considered catching John Ed in the act and putting an end to his thieving, but then, for the rest of his life, he'd feel ashamed and never again look her in the eye. She kept hoping he'd reform on his own.

A church stood on just about every block of Memphis — one for each tomfool person. There was also a bar on most every corner and she wondered why praying people would commit to living here.

John Ed came down the stairs to his room and shut the door. He hadn't been up there long enough to steal much if anything.

Friday was payday. He should have waited one more day. He wasn't any better at stealing than he was at playing harp. Why take a chance for little or nothing?

John Ed tried to copy a Little Walter tremolo—C harp, she guessed, and glory be almost got it down. Smiling to herself, she crumbed some day-old bread for topping the macaroni. Then the trucks pulled up the driveway and John Ed's tune soured.

Mack drove one truck, Rut the other. Mack gunned the motor and steered his truck through the porte-cochere, scraping the bricks on the house the same as every day—the buckets and ladders rattling and close behind, Rut honking his horn, a *hogwah* as mean as Little Walter's.

John Ed tried to imitate the sound—he hadn't the ear for it—and the noise he blew sputtered from his harp in what he'd admit was a "monotonic bust." Rene's ears rang and she wished for a tow sack full of cotton.

She opened the kitchen window to let out the steam, then wiped the foggy panes with a dishrag and watched Rut and the Uncles unload the trucks. She marveled how they'd come home without a speck of paint on their white painter's pants, shirts and caps. Sometimes she'd wonder if they had secret jobs and just pretended to paint.

Always they cleaned the equipment on the job site, but Rut was real particular about the brushes, and so for the second time they'd work the last flecks of paint out of the bristles with turpentine, paint thinner or water. She poked her head toward the screen and hollered about them puddling the concrete in front of the garage. They expected her to complain and she wouldn't disappoint them for the world.

Like a tribe of Neanderthals stirring soup, they hunkered over the buckets. A dot of color marked each lid, the color printed beside it — red, yellow, blue and fuchsia, a color she thought would be hard to look at all day long and who picked that one? Who could live with it?

Somebody either dying to be different or maybe color blind just like the Furies. Not one male Fury in all of history could tell blue from red. If left up to a Fury you'd have whole neighborhoods painted Crayola colors and none of them the wiser.

They began to argue over who'd get the first shower. Things hadn't changed much since their puberty, which had come all at once, like a fire storm.

Mack yelled, "Rene, send John Ed on out here to help us."

When did they begin calling her by her first name? She hadn't noticed when.

"He's working on his music!" she bellowed.

"We hadn't noticed," said Mel Ray, holding his ears.

"Hell to pay," grumbled Joe.

Then Franko, Joe's twin said, "Hell to pay," because he couldn't think up anything on his own. Franko had just enough sense to copycat was all. Set him to working and he'd go at it like a robot.

John Ed once made the mistake of pointing out Franko's deficiency to Joe.

"Get him painting on something and he just keeps laying it on in one spot. Okay with latex, but give him a bucket of semi-gloss and you got a mess on your hands."

Like John Ed really knew all about painting, or any kind of work for that matter.

Joe had defended Franko by knocking John Ed half way across the room. "Dedicated is what," he'd said, glaring at John Ed. "Something you don't know nothing about."

She felt John Ed had deserved his upbraid, but nobody could say he wasn't dedicated. Her ears were scorched from his dedication and just then she remembered the boiling greens.

"Rene, get the little Pisser to come load the extension ladder for tomorrow's job," yelled Mack.

She bristled at his bad talk, and would do no such

thing until he talked civil. She turned down the greens and the cabbage, walked to the back door and stepped outside to complain about the ugly talk. If you let a thing grow too big it's hard to trim it down.

"Londeen don't take to bad talk," said Rene, pointing to the house behind them. "It ain't right. Save some of that turpentine to clean up your tongues."

"Out in public the Uncles don't talk so bad," promised Rut.

"Londeen cusses like a sailor," said Mack. "You just think she don't."

Rene heaved a sigh. The low-hanging gray clouds seemed to touch the treetops, the first sign of snow, the stoop soon to be slippery from the drizzle. Rare to see snow in the South at all—and now so late in season. Almost spring. Wouldn't stick if it did snow.

Franko blew one time on his crow call. His blue eyes had a pleading look about them, his birdcall sounding that same way.

From atop the telephone pole the crow answered him. *Caw c-a-aw*! Franko knew something after all, the bird knew it too, and for a second she felt as light-hearted as a girl.

"Keep at it and you'll draw a sky full," said Mel Ray. "We got enough shit around here as it is, Franko."

Rene's bright mood dulled. She teetered on the stoop and sniffed the air, trying to get something back. "Albert Lily is burning his garbage again," and by the sudden deep tone of her own voice she felt she'd just issued him a citation. "It'll molder and stink when the rain starts back," she said and then caught the drift of her own garbage and held her nose.

Joe was watching her.

"Get fuzzy britches out here to take care of it," he said, flicking yellow water from his paint paddle onto Rene's compost heap half as high as the garage, and it ran in rivulets like lava from a volcano.

"Nothing will come up in the garden this year," she lamented.

"Paint water don't hurt nothing," he said.

Rene went back in the house and knocked on John Ed's door.

"Go on out and take care of the garbage. The Uncles are getting restless."

Her whole life she'd been able to hear the slightest sound — the peep of a baby chick under the house, the scurrying of cockroaches, her brothers whispering in their room, and from the outhouse, her mother's soft crying.

No one believed she'd heard a falling star land in a cloud net or a dirt dauber hissing. But now she heard nothing, not a fleck of sound from John Ed's room and she turned the knob and opened the door.

He was pitiful with the half grown goatee, not enough hair to sport one proper. He looked up at her like a calf at a new gate.

He had full red lips and big brown eyes and rusty hair that shined. Some girl would love him one day.

"You got to come on out. You can't hide in there forever."

He was looking at the floor, the harp squeezed so tight in his fist she heard it cry. "I can't get it down. It won't come out the way I know it ought to."

"If you believe in yourself, it don't matter what the others say."

"You can't stand it neither."

"I can stand it a while more. Until you learn it. Don't matter how long it takes. Now come on out."

In the kitchen she turned up the burners and heard him go out the back door. Okra picked and frozen from her garden in the summer, now drained in the colander.

You could chip a pod of okra from the center of an iceberg frozen one hundred years and it would still come out slimy as puss when it thawed. She scraped the carrot shavings onto a newspaper to save for the compost heap, wishing instead she could scrape off a few layers of her own skin, wishing she could feel new.

"Every last one of you is combustible," called Rut as he came in the back door. Mindful of his family history, he always insisted the Uncles strip off their shirts and hang them on pegs in the garage. In and out, life was a never-ending stream of men. Bare-chested and woolly as black sheep, slapping the goose bumps on their arms, they filed into the house behind him and clomped upstairs.

In the kitchen Rut took off his painter's cap and pecked Rene's cheek. "Dang," he said and she knew the uncles were wearing on him, his face a deep pink from being in charge of their lives. He put the cap back on his head, cocked it like a beret and went off to shower.

When he wasn't painting houses, he painted pictures of old abandoned shacks and barns. The lines on his face suggested regret. Because of the uncles or because he had to paint real houses to earn a living, she couldn't say.

She put the okra on to boil, started frying two strips of bacon to dress up the greens, checked the pork roast for doneness, set the cabbage on a trivet and used that same burner to heat up the black-eyed peas, adding a thin slice of country ham.

She removed the greens to a trivet, put on a pot of water for the potatoes, stirred the buttermilk into the cornbread mixture, and started peeling the potatoes.

She'd have to free up a burner for the green beans. She took out a jar of spiced peaches from the refrigerator, opened it and poured juice and fruit into a bowl.

She splashed vinegar into the greens, scattered capers over the buttery cabbage. She stuffed celery with a mixture of cream cheese and crushed pineapple, and pulled strings from the green beans and snapped them, fixing no more food than needed to keep their minds sound, bodies strong, and souls alive and full of hope.

Toweled at the waist, Rut shuffled into the kitchen in his maroon-colored terry slippers, his bird legs thin and white.

"Get John Ed to turn down that record," he said, taking an ice tray from the freezer and running it under the faucet. He plunked cubes in a glass and killed off his bottle of Evan Walker Red. "I can't hardly stand loud music so late in the day. I'm wore out."

"You need clothes on," said Rene. "You'll up and take sick."

It unnerved her to view Rut's old wiry body, not enough fat under his skin to protect his brittle bones. She adjusted all four burners and the oven's temperature. The music had an edge to it, sounded sassy.

"You don't like John Ed listening to Little Walter because the music's uppity or just too loud?"

"I like my harp pure," he said. "Like you'd hear in the old days before they miked it."

Sad Hours strutted out of the record player like a big rooster with his red comb held high as a king's crown—she could almost see feathers, the music so loud it shuddered the house and Rene clapped her hands over her ears and wished for a football helmet or a package of corks.

Rut downed his bourbon and sighed. "Better enjoy the tune while you can still make it out. Once John Ed gets his head full of it, it'll come shooting out of him like a firestorm."

At the supper table Rut kept trying to get John Ed talking. "John Ed, how's the pork?" "John Ed, could you stand another scoop of macaroni?" "John Ed, how's school?" Rut never understood that John Ed had used up all his air playing his music and didn't have enough left to blow out a candle.

The smorgasbord table groaned with the weight of steaming bowls and platters, each man serving himself and turning the wheel for the next. After the years of practice, they'd gotten it down about perfect.

"John Ed, if we get the job down at St. Patrick's Church, you might want to skip school some to help out," said Rut. "The pay is good and we could sure use you. It's a big job, bigger than most."

"This ain't no farm where you keep the youngsters home to pick seasonal," she said, cutting her ham into small bites. Rut wasn't much interested in education. She raised her voice a notch to make her point. "You know, this here's Memphis and there's expectations."

"I know what town I live in, Rene," said Rut. "I just think it might do John Ed good to work. I reckon I gave low bid."

"You always bid low," said Mack. "That's why we don't make money enough to get ahead."

"We do well enough."

"I need a mike real bad," said John Ed out of nowhere and everybody stopped eating and stared at him, all eyes on him like a hornet swarm. He bowed his head and prayed to his turnip greens.

Silence lowered the ceiling. Even Franko understood the implication, his droopy eyes suddenly wide open. He hawed with his mouth full, not a pretty sight. Joe held his head in hand.

Mack and Mel Ray gave each other the long lost brother look, which meant they were united in thought, word and deed.

Mack pointed his knife at John Ed. "You crazy, John Ed. You fuckin' crazy."

Mel Ray said, "We been entertained by you

enough as it is. You need to find someplace else to play. That ain't a request."

Rut reminded them the house was his and he'd make the decision on entertainment. "The discussion ain't open."

Joe hated loud voices. He began yammering about how Patsy Cline turned him on.

Rene stopped listening altogether. She went deep into her own thoughts. When Bill up and married Annie, not only did he join the Catholic Church to please her, but also the two of them became peaceniks and ran off to Canada. All that was left of them was a vase full of ashes and John Ed. He looked like a war orphan on a poster, just bigger was all. He was six years old when he'd first come here to live permanent.

Little as he was, Bill and Annie'd managed to brainwash him. At first he moped around about missing mass. At least they prayed in English now and Rene had tried to accommodate him, but she just couldn't take to a strange church and all that went with it—burning incense and worshipping saints.

Long before that happened—after the birth of the twins, which was God's dirty trick—Rene had given up religion altogether, otherwise she'd have settled John Ed into the Baptist Church. He was old enough now to pick any Christian religion he wanted, but she figured he'd forgotten all about it and here Rut was stirring him up to paint a Catholic church. She laughed hard at her own joke until she noticed them all looking at her.

She coughed into her napkin. Not one of them would ever guess what she thought about or what she knew. Between servings of cabbage and turnip greens she realized she wasn't really inside their circle. She could choose any trail she wanted—just go down it and no one the wiser. Wearing hiking boots on a trail leading nowhere in particular, that's how she imagined herself, and suddenly she felt a certain delight.

3

Pure sweetness never lasts.

Why couldn't she just accept it?

Mel Ray was honking the horn and out the door popped Mack growling about "missing five bucks" as he headed for the truck, in his hand one of her few matching coffee cups. Not so much as a *Thank you mother for the bountiful breakfast*, or *Hope you don't mind me running off with your prized coffee cup bought on your honeymoon in Gattlinburg*, or *See you at sundown*.

Mean-hearted and wishing the Uncles would go off on their own and take John Ed with them, she went on back inside.

It was a sin not to want your own progeny, but

there it was, and not just because they'd taken over the whole house. She hadn't much wanted them when they were little, either.

She felt like a shepherd put on this earth solely to tend to them. Certainly she hadn't applied for the job. She'd wanted to be a nurse and that's all she'd wanted to be. Come home after a shift and prop up her feet. Knit. Eat p-corn.

Maybe the Uncles would all get married in a group wedding and leave home together on the same day. Russian brides—they'd be the only women who'd accept a proposal from any of them. She'd soon get started on the paper work.

First she'd commit herself to being patient. It'd take time to convince even a deprived woman to take on one of them. Except Ruthie. Ruthie'd take Mack back in a New York second. Ruthie had it bad for Mack. But it was over now. Sadly over. *Volga Boatman.* She'd sing it to make the Russian brides feel at home.

Rene took money from the cookie jar, put it into her apron pocket and slipped down the hall to the door as stealthy as a Siamese cat. Up the airless stairway to the attic, she paused to admire the sign she'd posted.

CONDEMNED

Rut said she'd wasted her time ... the uncles took pride in her citation, which only encouraged them to knock down their standards.

She'd declared aloud she wouldn't cross the threshold of their room until they scrubbed the place. They courted filth just to keep her out.

She opened the door and stepped into what looked to be a fugitive's shack in the woods along the Mississippi River. Not even a fugitive would want to live in it. The corner bathroom, such as it was—sink, crapper and shower—was separated from the rest of the room by Rut's old moth-eaten army blanket from World War II hung from a clothesline.

Lined up on the shelf were the unused Ajax, Mr. Clean, and Zud she'd bought for them along with the unopened cans of air fresheners: essences of lavender, musk, wisteria, bayberry, clove, and pine, not one of them powerful enough to keep down the odors in the first place.

Rene held her breath and edged around Mack's bed covered in a hill of blankets. Each uncle had claimed territory, arranging the furniture as boundary lines. She felt the trepidation of a poacher crossing a bobbed wire fence onto posted land. She did not want to get caught in the room she'd vowed never to enter. Next to Mack's bed stood his icebox loaded with beer—Schmidt for every day, quarts of regular Miller for weekends and six packs of Schlitz for special occasions.

Whenever Mack claimed to be a connoisseur of beer, Rut would say, "Connoisseur of cheap."

Hell to pay, Mack rotated his stock in such a way that he'd notice a missing beer — a battalion he called it: Schmidts the ground troops, Schlitzes the officers, Millers the army brass. He'd down a Schmidt from the top shelf, then replace it with a reserve Schmidt from the bottom shelf, rarely moving the Millers from behind the lines or the Schlitzes from the flank. Mack got out of Vietnam without getting shot. He had scars no one else could see.

A draft between the dormer and the little porthole window in the bathroom corner stirred the odors. Holding her nose, Rene took a can of air freshener from the shelf and sprayed pine scent until she felt lightheaded and full of artificial forest.

She took a Schmidt from the icebox, popped the top, and drank some to clear her head. The first beer is either the best or the worst, Mack always said. Rene chugged down the worst beer she'd ever tasted and burped loudly.

Rut said he'd lost respect for Schmidt when it froze before the milk did, but Rut was a caution and she knew his criticism had more to do with the volume Mack drank than the quality of the beer. Rut had served in World War II, old for a volunteer, but the army took him anyhow.

He'd fought the Japanese, but mostly he blamed the Germans for the war, and now, more than twenty years after the surrender, he still resented how Hitler's men had come over to America and took over everything from brewing beer to building bombs just like they owned the place. They pretended to be as American as the Germans who'd had sense enough to come earlier. He'd said the Germans would get you in trouble — they'd get you in a fight or get you drunk. Rene thought Americans drank and fought because they loved it and needed no encouragement from anybody else, least of all the Germans.

She helped herself to another Schmidt and worried over the uncles' drinking and fighting in bars. What worried her even more was fire in the attic. When the uncles got all of the heaters going at once, it looked like Hell up here, a red hot fiery Hell threatening the whole house and everybody in it — just burn the whole place down and not leave any identifiable remains.

Throughout time members of the Fury clan had gone up in flames, so often, in fact, that death by fire was considered a family curse. Rut himself experienced a near miss in the mule barn fire. Full proof of the curse came from Bill and Annie.

Their fiery deaths had left Rene with the helpless feeling she constantly fought against—that sooner or later the whole family would burn up. Except for herself. Her skin was thick, almost asbestos, and worse than burning alive, she'd be left as the family witness.

She'd tried to prepare them for an emergency by blowing a whistle for the fire drill. Instead of calmly walking single file downstairs to the outside, they hung out the dormer windows singing *Hot Time in the Old Town Tonight*, a caterwauling that stirred the whole neighborhood.

Rut sighed and said they might as well learn all the verses.

At first sign of spring—the upstart of dandelions meant spring—Rut unplugged the space heaters in the attic. As soon as he'd put them away, instantly the lines on his old worn face smoothed out. Her own face in the mirror would ease some too, and maybe this year the crow's feet around her eyes would fly away!

She brushed a stray hair from her forehead, the feel of her ruddy, rough skin and the years gone by. She and Rut were too old to manage a houseful of men plus John Ed, and just to prove it, here she sat drinking beer, mulling over her life, and covering up John Ed's sins. Her own salvation was doubtful at best. The blind leading the blind.

She wished Bill and Annie would suddenly appear and take John Ed off their hands. She wished the Russian brides would suddenly come knock on the door and claim her sons.

She picked up Mack's El Producto cigar box from the top of his refrigerator, put in the five dollars to cover John Ed's debt, and set the box back again, then counted out dollar bills for Franko, Joe, and Mel Ray, guessing at the amounts, and in between sips of Schmidt, worried over a grandson who might well serve time in the pen if he wasn't careful.

In some place like Brushy Mountain or Parchman with wild Negroes carrying hidden switch blades and white trash so low born they lived only to sin, he'd really get the blues. She was surprised one of her own sons ... Mack or Mel Ray ... hadn't been in juvenile detention or prison, but Mel Ray'd straightened up as he grew and the army had calmed down Mack.

The dormers allowed the northern light into the room. From up here Mack sometimes shot squirrels out of the oak trees with his twenty-two. He'd fitted it with a silencer so that it gave off only a ping sound. Back and forth the crows would caw a peculiar funereal sound.

It was against the law to shoot in the city, but the neighbors never complained, never seemed to notice the dead squirrels littering the streets. She guessed the neighbors were afraid to complain to a man with a panther tattooed from his right shoulder to his wrist, a panther made alive by his hairy arm.

When John Ed first came to live with them, he took a look at Mack's arm, and still in the dream-like trance of a displaced person, he swore he heard that old panther growl.

"It did," he insisted. "It *did*."

Around the table everybody—Rut, Mel Ray, Joe, Rene, even Franko, sat droop-jawed and stonily silent, until Mack flexed his arm and the panther's mouth widened. Rene heard it growl, but didn't admit it— the others all hard laughing at John Ed.

She held off telling it because she was afraid Rut might commit her to the loony bin. She looked at John Ed and held her eyes to him just to let him know she believed him.

Now she looked at the pictures of women stuck to the walls, mostly in various stages of undress, and she remembered John Ed's old dream told to her just after he'd come to stay. It happened on a night when the uncles let him sleep up here.

Next morning he woke Rene up and pulled her upstairs to look at the picture of the woman with dark eyes and long, curly dark hair, near image of Annie.

In his dream, the woman floated from the picture to his bed, hovering over him in the dark room, quiet and calm, and he heard the chink of her Indian beads and felt the air stir around him.

A fingertip pressed *V* on his chest, filling his head and heart with peace. The dark haired woman, yellowed now, still hung above Joe's bed, the magic gone out of her long ago.

Not one of Joe's women wore a bikini or even a plunging neckline, his standards miles higher than Mack's, Mel Ray's or Franko's, who considered naked women on filling station calendars the same as the Mona Lisa when anybody with sense knows those eyes say things a woman dumb enough to be photographed in her birthday suit couldn't even think up.

Mack and Mel Ray razed Joe for keeping the flashlight beside his bed for shining on the women whenever he woke in the middle of the night. He ignored his brothers and kept on shining.

"Sweet women make sweet dreams," he'd say.

Rene thought Joe looked at their pictures because he lacked the imagination to dream up sweet women on his own.

She placed one dollar in Joe's jar and five in Franko's. Except for Franko, they'd all opened back accounts, but hardly ever deposited money because they didn't want Uncle Sam to know they had any. She figured someday Franko would become rich because he couldn't think up anything other than bird calls to spend his money on.

Though Rene wouldn't admit it except to herself, the "o" in Franko's name stood for zero. Being a twin to Joe was the kindly hand of fate for Franko. Not that you'd mistake Joe for a brain or anything, but you'd consider him a finished piece of work. You'd see Franko and Joe standing together, the two of them so much alike on the outside you'd just automatically figure twin brains and Franko got credit for having more sense than he was due.

His crow calls hung from hooks on the wall. Each morning he'd choose one to wear around his neck day long. Rene counted thirty-three calls on the wall, one for each day of the month plus extras. After watching a demonstration at a sporting goods store, he'd saved up and bought them all at once. At first nobody in the Fury family could figure why so many.

"Not that many crows live in Memphis," Rut had said, scratching his head.

All along Rene understood each crow had a tone of its own, same as the crow calls, though you had to listen close to hear it.

Until the day Franko first got going and gave off a couple of stiff ones, Rene had never seen a crow within five miles of the city limits. All of a sudden a murder of crows flew over and landed in the tops of the tallest trees — the sycamore, the black gums and the oaks, and cawed their heads off. It was the same almost every time Franko blew the call—the gathering of crows in the neighborhood some sort of family reunion. Because of the racket and because of the droppings, the neighbors would carp—Londeen about the droppings, Albert Lily about the noise.

If she or Rut didn't interrupt Franko with supper or a chore, he'd blow his guts out, calling crows until the flesh fell off his bones. He understood bird talk better than English, and she guessed he held faithfully to cawing—so much so he once peed his pants—because the crows understood him, too.

The crows knew he wasn't trying to fool them like some others. When she heard the caws going back and forth between Franko and the crows, Rene figured she was witness to some kind of magic. She couldn't say just what it meant, only that it meant something. She marveled how the sky would darken whenever the crows came.

From the open window a snow breeze stirred the top magazine on Mel Ray's rack. Across the way Londeen's roof was snow-covered. Rene put several dollars in Mel Ray's jar sitting on top of his old jukebox full of 45s that stood in one corner of the room. Mel Ray got high on music recorded in Memphis by Sam Phillips down at S.U.N.—Elvis, Johnny Cash and Jerry Lee Lewis.

The uncles all craved songs about fire, went nuts over Cash's "Ring of Fire," and bigger fools for Lee's "Great Balls of Fire," and turned up the volume so loud the whole house rattled with piano trills. Rene would accuse them of tempting fate with their fire music. She'd threaten not to cook another meal until they turned it off.

Mel Ray and Mack told the story about how Jerry Lee stopped in at the Nitelighter after midnight and played with Moetta.

"Long about two a.m. he got a hard on and tore up the piano. Smashed it to smithereens!"

Every time Mel Ray and Mack talked about the wild Jerry Lee, Franko and Joe would clap and hoot the same as if they'd been there, which they hadn't. Rene thought they all loved how Jerry Lee destroyed things more than they loved his music.

Mel Ray's jar looked a tad light, so she put in another dollar, then scanned the songs on the jukebox, mostly Jerry Lee and Elvis. She puzzled over why the uncles rarely listened to anything recorded after 1960, as if they'd got stuck in time. Here it was 1968 — all music recorded in stereo now — and the uncles still monaural.

When John Ed played his Little Walter's too loud, Mel Ray would threaten to use them for skeet practice, so it surprised Rene to find Little Walter's "Juke" on the jukebox. She wished she had a nickel for every time she'd listened to that song downstairs, and now half of it played through her head before she could stop it.

She stood in the center of the room and looked up to see what new stuff the uncles had sniffed out at garage sales—always on the last day when nothing but junk was left. A new picture of President Johnson pulling his dogs' ears hung from the rafters below Mack's beer signs—*Schmidt, Miller, Schlitz*.

"Higgledy piggledy," Rene said aloud.

Nailed along the eaves were the same old rusty tools, coon tails, a picture of an Indian speared in the heart and dying, pieces of bobbed wire, a passel of railroad spikes, a rare souvenir photo of Elvis wearing a coon skin cap, more calendar prints of naked women, a political poster of Estes Kefauver wearing a coon skin cap, fishing rods, glass insulators from telephone poles, a photo of Fess Parker wearing a coonskin cap, a picture of the Beatles wearing hard hats, a hornets' nest, and the skins and heads of animals they'd killed in the woods when they hunted: three deer—two bucks and a doe—a raccoon, and a coyote.

The doe looked down at Rene with sad gray eyes. She hoped John Ed's stealing would come to an end before she did, but also felt oddly comforted to know his head was full of music, something alive. Never mind she couldn't listen to his harp without flinching.

She turned to one of Rut's paintings hung up there. "A failure," he'd called it. "The sky's too blue." So blue, she thought, you'd hardly notice the house, as

good as a house gets to her way of thinking. Rut made the same blue-sky mistakes so often she agreed when he called his heavy-handedness a "sin of excess."

"It's like this," he'd say. "Franko here caws too much, Mack drinks too much, John Ed plays his harmonica too much. And Rene, I hate to say it, but you cook too much. Whatever gets out front and leads you by the nose — that's excess."

Then he'd ponder over the first part before adding the ending. "I ain't saying I specifically worry over sin all that much. You don't have to spend time puzzling over what naturally dogs at your heels. If you want to see what I'm saying, take a look at this here house and pay particular attention to the blue sky above it."

His hand drew an arc in the air above the house so you'd naturally think of a rainbow when no such thing ever showed up in his painting — mind you, he couldn't paint a raindrop or a rainbow either one if he had to — then he'd stand aback gazing at his sky.

She could see his excess plain and simple and

didn't need convincing, but sin or no sin, some things a person just couldn't control. Rut could no more quit painting too blue than John Ed could quit playing blues harp. And they weren't the only ones. Franko would dry up and blow away if he couldn't talk to crows—the evidence of his excess plain enough on the step, metal yard chairs, and the driveway. Beer eased Mack of what ailed him, though he sometimes drank enough to become comatose as a slug in sun. With her own head dulled with beer, she couldn't think what excesses Mel Ray and Joe were guilty of—garage sales maybe—their plunder evidence enough.

When the time was right she'd let them all know with a little excess of her own. She'd buy a different colored broom for each of them. Otherwise, they might not catch her drift. Instead of nagging, she'd simply hand out the brooms. "Clean sweep," she'd tell them and never look back.

4

Rain, snow or heat, everyone did as they pleased on Saturdays, coming and going at all hours and dishing up chili or stew directly from the pot on the stove when it suited them. Saturdays, she wasn't in charge. She didn't count heads. These things Rene would contemplate on Sunday, after the familiar loud rap rattled the front door.

"Okay Ruth Anne," hollered Rene.

She took up her sewing basket, slipped her arm through the handle as if someone might steal it, and shuffled to the front door. She opened it to Ruthie who stood there pretty as you please in a short black skirt and eye-burning red top.

"Ruth Anne, you know good and well we ain't formal here. You park in back. You come in back. Just like the rest of the family."

"I ain't family no more, Rene."

Uh, oh. Ruthie was about to pop out of that top tight as skin. She'd have Mack swallowing his tongue. "You look hot, Ruth Anne." She hoped Ruthie didn't take it the way she'd meant it. It was going to be one of those days.

"Mack's out back, Ruth Anne."

"I came to see you, Rene. I got something to tell you. No need to get Mack and them riled up."

She looped her arm through the handle of Rene's sewing basket, their arms touching, and together they walked down the hall into the kitchen and set it on the table. "What you got in here Rene? Hedge Shears?"

"Just about."

Ruthie looked out the window toward the row of Rut and the Uncles sitting bare-chested in the sun.

"Just look at the heat rising from that bunch. Some things never change."

Rene poured Ruthie a cup of coffee and one for herself and they sat down at the yellow Formica table, stirring and sipping in silence. Rene had missed Ruthie's springy black hair, her blue eyes clear as morning. Most of all she'd missed their woman talk. The soft days were gone now.

Ruthie had a wild streak nobody could control. Put her and Mack together drinking beer and they'd fight about something every time. When love got busted, hardly ever did the pieces fit back together. Still, Rene wished it would happen. The two of them lived no better apart than together.

Ruthie looked at her.

"John Ed was in Green's last night. I took him home and put him to bed on my couch. This morning he was gone."

You counted on Ruth Anne not to waste time telling things. She'd get right to the point, letting you fill in the blanks.

"Ruthie, somehow John Ed managed to get on home," she insisted. "Leastwise he was here when I went in to check on him this morning."

Rene set down her cup and headed to John Ed's room.

"Rise and shine," she said and pulled back the lump of covers in John Ed's bed, recognizing the fool that was herself. The weight of the world pressed down on her shoulders.

Back in the kitchen again, she sat down heavily.

"Colored place, Ruth Anne?"

"Mr. Green don't mind us coming in." Ruthie tossed the hair back over her ear. "Wouldn't be nothing wrong with John Ed soaking up music, only he's underage and the police get rough if they catch a white boy in a black establishment."

"You mean juke joint, don't you, Ruth Anne? Why don't Green just tell John Ed he can't come in? Put an end to it."

"John Ed got Joe's identification. I hate to be the one to rat on him, but it ain't hardly fair to Mr. Green. He runs a real nice place. Not many fights. John Ed pretending to be Joe ain't right for sure. You got to handle this one, Rene. Without telling Mack and them."

"I can't hardly accommodate a thief, Ruth Anne, but him losing his folks so young and me not having the get up and go to do right by him … John Ed's had it rough. I'm too old, Ruth Anne."

"You'll work it out, Rene. I know you will."

"Joe ain't even noticed his driver's missing."

"That don't surprise me. Joe ain't much brighter than Franko."

"At least he don't drink in juke joints. Beer parlors, maybe. I guess they ain't much difference.

Ruth Anne, you going out with a Negro?"

"I ain't dating nobody, Rene. If I was, it wouldn't be nobody's business."

Rene raised her shoulders, let them fall.

"You ain't without sympathy, Rene."

"I just don't do my drinking with Negroes. Drinking oils the tongue. Things get said. How am I going to find John Ed?"

"When he gets hungry, he'll come on home."

"The boy eats like a bird."

"You could do with a vacation, Rene."

She was looking at the clean dishes in the dish drain and the dirty pots soaking in the sink.

"You work like a slave for a houseful of grown men. They ought to be tending to themselves."

Ruthie sipped coffee from a spoon.

"At least you got heart, Rene. That's more than I can say for that oldest son of yours."

"Mack ain't all that bad. He hadn't settled into life just yet."

"He'd better hurry up before it's all over. You, too, Rene."

"Ain't a day goes by I don't have commitments. Today I got to shear."

"See what I mean?"

"At least it'll keep my mind off John Ed. You got to help me, Ruth Anne. I just can't go it alone today."

Ruth Anne heaved a sigh. "I vowed I'd never shear another Fury as long as I lived."

Rene stood to pick up her sewing basket and headed to the back door.

"You didn't really mean it though."

Outside Mel Ray lay in the hammock.

"Ruthie, Baby." He shifted his weight, enough to set the hammock swaying. Franko and Joe looked up from the comic books they were reading and smiled at her. Rut set down his paper. "Just in time, Ruth Ann."

Ruthie patted his hand like you do some oldster. Mack bounced his spring chair and looked to the sky as if something were falling, his chin bobbing in the rhythm of some song in his head. He stole a look at Ruthie as she sat down at on the old round metal table decorated with a giant sunflower decoupage she and Rene had done together. Ruthie pretended not to feel his eyes, but Rene heard love crackle and was surprised no one else seemed to.

She settled herself in a chair and started digging in her sewing basket, finding stuff she hadn't seen since last spring—ribbons, needles and the buttons she'd salvaged from worn-out clothes.

Franko hovered over her shoulder, a raccoon plucking out anything shiny—a thimble, an upholstery needle, a crochet hook. She allowed him, but only under her supervision.

He was partial to the old wooden spools she'd saved and held up one wound with fluorescent pink thread. His eyes twinkled as he showed it to Ruthie and Rene. "Might be a good color for the house, Franko," encouraged Rene half-heartedly. The paint on their own house was peeling and Rut not the least interested in the necessary repairs. "Better pink than no paint at all."

Rut slumped in his chair, the subject of painting the house draining all the life from his body. "She never gives up, Ruthie."

"Maybe one day she'll up and choose a color that suits you, Rut. You'd all be the better for it."

"Pink from purple, they can't tell the difference," mumbled Rene. While she wanted to keep Rut on the subject of painting the house, she knew when to let a thing go. "Time for the annual," she said. "Ruthie's helping. Just like old times."

"Wouldn't have missed it for the world," said Ruthie under her breath.

"I don't believe that for one minute, Ruthie," said Rut. "But it's nice you're willing to help civilize the world. Let's get on with it."

Ruthie had no more than picked up the scissors when Joe's hope of being the chosen one spilled out of him. "Halleluiah!" he hollered, suddenly alert for the first time in recent memory.

Rene gave him a hard frown and held it on him like a hot iron. His face turned the deep purple. She looked from son to son and in a loud voice announced,

"This here's Shearing Day. Nothing more."

Franko nervously fiddled with his crow call. Rut cautioned him not to blow it.

"We ain't ready for the crows just yet, Franko. We got hair to cut."

Mel Ray coolly rubbed his hairy stomach, putting in his bid for Ruthie. Rene looked at Rut who caught on. He lowered his head. It took a man's voice to get their attention and end his sons' tug-of-war over Ruthie.

"This ain't the ruttin' season—it's the velvet stage."

"Some of it's velvet. Some's not," said Ruthie, glancing at the hairy chests. Damn if she wasn't keeping the whole thing going and Rene not knowing how to stop her.

His chair screeching concrete, Mack turned his back on them all and started blowing smoke rings. "It ain't necessary for you to get involved with the hair of this family, Ruth Anne. Some things a man keeps private."

"Private?" she said. Her own red lips seemed to blow smoke, though she'd quit cigarettes months back with the help of a hypnotist. Ruthie had a yearning for things exotic. Most recent she'd discovered a walk-in acupuncture clinic in South Memphis. They'd taken her in quick as you please and eased the inflamed bunion she'd gotten from wearing the spiked heels she refused to give up. Rene didn't understand the necessity of raising yourself up so high up from the ground. Like you was a stilt walker.

"Private?" she said again, and stood up to spread her arms toward Londeen's house. "Nothing you do out here is private." She rocked up on the tip of her toes, her red top and all that was in it bobbling. "All of you out here half naked and it don't take a crow to see what you're up to for God's sake. It's a sheep shearing festival. Invite the world! Set up concessions. Hire a band! Get a Johnny-on-the Job."

"My life's private," said Mack, sullen as never before. "I got other interests now, Ruthie."

"Who? Some old crusty bar bitch down at the Axel Grease with dyed black hair who thinks she's Patsy Cline reincarnated? Picking her way through a second miserable life?"

"We both know all about miserable."

Keeping order, Rene lined up several pairs of scissors according to size. "Ruthie's gone and spit a mouthful," she whispered to Rut who nodded.

Now Mack stood face to face with Ruthie. "Mind your own business is what I'm saying."

Ruthie jabbed toward his stomach with her long red fingernail and Rene wondered if it was sharp as it looked. Some folks were better kept apart—separate beds, houses, and lives.

Londeen came out of her house and started in gathering clothespins from her line, hair pulled back for eavesdropping. Londeen didn't believe in working on Sunday, but to her, pin-gathering didn't count as work. She saw Rene looking and came toward the fence.

"I saw a rat," she said. "Right there on that compost heap of yours, Rene. King of the hill. You see one rat, there's a hundred more hiding out. Pestilence isn't far behind. In the dark of night rats will burrow into this neighborhood and live like kings. It's all in the Bible."

"I'm afraid of rats," said Ruthie, holding pair of scissors with both hands as if she might plunge the blades into anything that came near. Mack noticed and sat back down.

"I don't pretend to understand much about this labor union—Irish Commies from what I know—but if all the sanitation workers go on strike this compost heap of yours means property devaluation. This whole city becomes a garbage dump. Rats will rule!"

"I ain't seen a one," said Rut.

"Londeen, you could stand a trim," said Rene,

peering purposely at her old bleached blonde head and not one bit sorry Londeen was outnumbered by six today.

"You see here," said Londeen. Without invitation, she picked up a stick and came through the gate, pointing to depressions in the compost heap. "That's rat tracks … vermin all over the place. Rene Fury, I've seen you throw food scraps on this heap and that's why we got us an invasion of rats." She poked her stick into one of the depressions. "Step back because something's liable to run out."

"Londeen, you're working overtime," said Mack.

Londeen ignored him as she ignored most opinions save her own. "I admit John Ed keeps 'um down with his harmonica playing. High pitched noise will do it every time.

Drives a rat crazy. On the other hand, crow poop gives a rat something to eat even if you didn't have this heap. You'd do well to get John Ed out here to play some more awful music — get rid of the rats and crows at the same time. Course you'd have to stop Franko from calling crows in the first place and that ain't likely to happen with his sort of dilemma of the mind."

Busy looking up at the sky, Franko didn't seem to hear Londeen. Not one crow was in sight and he seemed sad because of it.

Rene couldn't imagine asking him to give up the one thing he loved. Better for him to remain ignorantly happy and cawing his head off. She envied him that.

"Give a blow, Franko. They're around here somewhere."

Londeen's face was screwed up in a frown. "You been listening to me, Rene?"

Rene refused to acknowledge one blamed thing Londeen said. About rats or anything else. "You want your haircut or not, Londeen?"

"Not on your life," said Londeen, and she marched back through the gate. It sprang forward and slapped her on the butt. She held her head erect and acted as if nothing had happened. "Yesterday the crows stole my clothespins right off the line. My clothes fell down in the dirt. I had to wash every single thing all over again."

"Hard job with a wringer washer," said Mel Ray.

"I've got myself a fine-running modern machine, Mel Ray. You keep your jokes to yourself. I might be poor, but I ain't impoverished."

"Londeen, I saw a big crow wearing a pink nightgown," said Mack. "That wouldn't be yours, would it?"

Londeen pursed her lips, behind which you could see half a grin. "When you git bit, you'll think twice,

Mack Fury."

Rene refused to cotton to Londeen about the rats or anything else. "The offer's still good, Londeen. We're likely to be out here cutting hair for a good while."

"Not on your life," said Londeen.

Straightaway she walked up her back steps and into her house, slamming the backdoor behind her.

"Lordy." On the table Rene lined up three pairs of shears and a pair of small scissors. From the garage Rut brought the hedge trimmers and the grass clippers and sprayed the mechanisms with WD-40, scissoring the air to work in the oil.

"Give us a hand, Franko. Bring me a rake and the broom." Rut's voice carried weight even if what he said was ordinary. "Pass the biscuits," or "I'm tuckered" or "I might get me another dog."

When you didn't hear much of nothing from him, you valued whatever finally came out, as if it were worth money.

Franko let loose of his call long enough to fetch a broom, a rake and the ax he promptly dropped with a clang on the concrete.

"We don't allow weapons at the clipping, Franko. You done forgot the story."

Rut talked slow and loud so Franko would never forget. "Ax, sickle, ice pick. Those three things we got no use for on shearing day." Then he retold the old story of how he'd caught Mack and Mel Ray dueling with ice picks when they were kids, how hard it had been to bust them up, how they admitted they'd already gone a round or two with the sickle and the ax. Nobody got hurt or killed, but the thought of it still got on Rut's nerves. You could always tell. "Best to keep those three things out of sight and mind," he mumbled.

"Amen," said Rene, remembering her own anxiety, and again she felt it in her face, the lines lengthening and tightening, her mouth drawn down like an old mad-faced frog. That day she'd been hopping mad.

Rut picked up the ax and stood it against the garage. "It's best to keep such tools where they're not so handy." He sat down and started in sharpening a pair of Rene's scissors.

"What about getting started? If I'm to help Rene, I want to get going on it."

Mack scowled. "It ain't none of your business, Ruthie. You ain't attached here no more."

"I hope that ain't never the case," said Rut. "Wouldn't ever get done with the shearing without Ruthie. Let's get on with it."

Ruthie sucked her quivering lip and started in clipping Franko's back with a pair of Rene's sewing

186

scissors. He was sitting in a folding chair and he shivered a little when she touched him.

She ran her hand back and forth across his back, steadying him some. Joe held his own head with the butt of his hand, Mel Ray somber, both of them jealous as all get out.

"You got more hair than a bear," said Ruthie. She cut body hair in a style and method all her own, clipping one row at a time, top to bottom, then stood back to determine if it was short enough. If it wasn't, she'd have another go at it. "You know, Franko. I swear your hair grows while I'm cutting it."

"That ain't the only thing growing," said Mel Ray, sounding bitter, wishing it was himself growing.

By the sweet expression on Franko's smiling face, with his hands folded in his lap, he looked to be praying for his hair to keep on growing so she'd keep on cutting.

"Oo ... whee!"

It was Joe hollering. Rene worked on him, carefully cutting the sparse hair around the perimeter of his chest, slowly working her way toward the wooly middle.

"Careful there, Mother Rene. That's some hard cold steel."

"Stainless," she bragged. "Keep talking. It's nice to know you got a voice."

"Them's German scissor," said Rut. "Have to admit the Germans is good at tool making." Rut sharpened the trimmers with his snake stone. "I'll have to do this two or three times before it's over with. Don't take long for wiry hair to dull the tools."

"You can take care of my back first," said Mel Ray, and he flopped over on the hammock, almost spilling himself out of it, rocking back and forth as he got himself situated in the middle. "I don't want no hair sprouting out of my collar. I might be getting a date tonight." He was looking at Ruthie who refused to return his gaze.

"I got the job of mowing you," said Rut. "Ruthie can trim you some."

"That'll take a sickle," said Mack. "Mel Ray's got a stand of Johnson grass."

Mel Ray's furry hair fell to the ground in thick tufts. "You could sell this stuff," said Rut. "Or put it in the compost."

"Does seem a waste," said Rene. "Growing all this hair for nothing." Joe's hair covered her legs up to her calves. She felt like a gooney bird too big for its nest. "Toupees or pillow stuffing, maybe. Or pot scrubbers. We'd have enough hair for thousands if we was to make 'um small."

"Franko's is too soft for scrubbing," said Ruthie in her sexy blue voice. She kicked at the hair falling on her feet. "Get the sticky out of it and it might make a chamois."

"Not this stuff," said Rut. He'd started in on Mack's fur with the hedge trimmers. "Maybe if you boiled it down some." He held a tuft of hair in his fingers and examined it. "You know you're getting grizzly, son?"

"There's an art to this," said Rene."

"You're good all right," said Rut.

"I hereby declare you a pro."

The snip of the clippers and shears kept a steady pace and hair fell like summer wheat or hay in harvest. Franko wanted to blow his crow call and Ruthie stopped him just as he put it to his lips, his cheeks ruddy from holding the air for the blast.

"Let go of it," said Rene, worried that he'd cut off air to his brain or hyperventilate.

"I dreamed about plowing last night," Rut said. "You was right there next to me in the middle, Mack. On either side of us was Mel, Joe, Franko, Bill and John Ed, all of us together. Each of us had a mule and we plowed seven rows abreast. The dust rose up behind the plows, and right then the dream turned the same Nut Brown as on True Life's color chart. Each of us grinned like we had good sense. The mules, too. Showed off their teeth and gums."

"Mules look that way just before they bite," said

Mack. "If mule don't bite, it's just because it forgot how."

"No, sir. Everyone of the mules in my dream was plain thrilled to take part in plowing."

Stunned, that's what Rene was ... because she'd dreamed Rut's dream, or because he'd dreamed hers? Maybe the dream was so big it couldn't fit into Rut's head and seeped into her own.

Or vice versa. He'd identified the faces the way she'd done, and the dust-covered mules and plows. Married too long, she guessed, so long they weren't able to keep from merging one into the other, joined at the head like Siamese twins.

She'd wait until no one else was around before she told Rut. When he found out about the shared dream, she felt sure it would puzzle him for a long time to come.

"Just a few wild hairs," said Rut and he laughed at his own joke and nobody else did. "Let Ruthie snip these few, Mack."

"Pass on that," said Mack.

"Most likely Ruthie's altogether tired of cutting hair," said Rene, her eyes slowly crisscrossing back and forth from Rut to Ruthie, and she felt her patience winding down like a clock.

She wondered about marriage, about losing yourself in another person, and maybe that wasn't a good thing after all. Maybe Mack and Ruthie ought to leave well enough alone. First dream-sharing, then everyday thoughts.

Where would it end? Maybe you'd become invisible to yourself—look in the mirror and see your better half staring back at you.

"Sit here, Joe," said Ruthie, motioning to a metal spring chair. "This'll only take a few snips. You ain't quite as hairy as your brothers."

Uh, oh. Insult. Rene hoped nothing more would be said about hair, men are such babies about such things, so fragile and wan about all of it. If a man didn't have as much of something as another man he might as well be impotent. Everything had to do with those seeds. Whether or not they had abundance. Hair didn't make a hill of beans, she wanted to say. Otherwise, she'd have more than one grandchild, God forbid.

"I'm gettin' up some of this before it takes over."

Rene picked up a broom, sweeping the hair from around the chair legs and off her own feet into piles, and soon it grew as big and round as a basketball.

"Would you look a that," said Rene. She prodded the big black ball with her foot and set it rolling. "I never in my life thought it'd stick together like that. Mel Ray, what kind of hair oil you using?"

"No reason for it sticking together. None of us

use hair cream," said Mel Ray. "Unless you call *cream* whatever in hell's name Franko rubs on his head."

Franko felt his hair. It was true he sprayed it every morning with God-only-know-whatever can sat on the basin—deodorant or air freshener, flavoring his hair with peppermint or scenting it with pine. Nobody talked or cut while the hairball traveled. It rolled in the light spring wind, picking up leaves, dirt, twigs, and grass.

"Tumbleweed," said Rut. He pulled down some long strands of hair before his eyes and snipped them. Then he walked over to scatter them on the tumbleweed.

To Rene it seemed much more, and she regretted not being part of it, but her hair was thinning and she figured she'd better keep what she had.

"We're needing to get this project finished," said Rut, and he earnestly began clipping Mack's hair.

"This how they do it in Scotland?" asked Mel Ray just for something to say.

"They probably go at it a little more determined than us," said Rut. "Course they got more sheep."

This got Ruthie to laughing, and she blew the clipped hair from Franko's neck, him shivering hard as goose bumps popped up and covered his skin.

Mack looked away from Ruthie, his face flushed. When she laughed, he seemed stirred up and uneasy, his foot tapping impatiently when Rut started his slow talking drawl.

"You ever seen a sheep's eyes?" asked Rut. "Got a shy love-making look about 'um. I'm saying they're plain sweet."

"What about black sheep?" asked Joe.

"Black sheep got sweet black eyes last time I looked," said Rut.

"Ain't that the truth," said Ruthie, and she looked at Mack, her breasts heaving up and down like a robin's. Pity she herself couldn't fly.

Rut was match-making Ruthie and Mack with all his sheep talk. Mack's dull blue eyes *were* hooded like a sheep's, but weren't nothing sweet about him. Rut should leave well enough alone. Ruthie's eyes were full of fire. She was the one stood to lose.

While Rut brushed him with a whisk broom, Mack sat rigid, then stood up. "I'm gonna sun myself before I shower off," he said.

Ruthie sidled up to him and stood there, arm over arm and clutching the edge of her top. Rene worried she might to pull it over her head, the day growing warmer by the minute. Ruthie looked Mac straight in the eye and half whispered, "Talk to me before you get yourself dressed."

"Ruthie," said Mack in a hushed voice. "You done took up with the wrong sort of folks."

"You're into one of those old bar grits. We both know that's playing with fire."

"I just ain't into you, Ruthie."

With a mound of sorrow in her heart, Rene looked away from Ruthie. Mack might as well have knocked her to the ground. Tears welled in her eyes. She was coming apart like a rag doll when the seams split and all the stuffing falls out.

"You was married to a bear, Ruthie. You're free now," said Rene, holding her anger inside. "Free as a little bird."

"More than one sheep in this world, Ruthie," said Rut, looking half-ashamed.

Ruthie smiled, and with the side of her shoe, she gave the tumbleweed a push toward the driveway and watched it roll to a stop under the portico. Her eyes glazed over and she started to cry.

Mack was a sucker for tears. His own eyes began to water.

Ruthie snuffled then held her breath until finally she got hold of herself. Mack picked up his shirt and handed it to her and she blotted around her eyes and had the good sense not to wipe mascara on it. She wiggled her shoulders and got herself straight.

He took her by the arm, and together, they walked under the portico. Mack picked up the tumbleweed and rolled it toward the backyard like a bowling ball. It stopped at the foot of Rene's compost heap. Ruthie hummed some lowdown blues Rene didn't know and she guessed at the words without hearing them.

Too old to understand lovemaking, Rene was ready for them to do it somewheres else. "Mack, there's beer in the bottom of the refrigerator."

Franko was hard watching with more than a little interest. Rene didn't want him thinking about sex. At least John Ed wasn't here to witness what would make a young boy horny and then some.

Mack and Rene suddenly stopped like folks on a cake walk when the music quits, then up and kissed each other as if the whole world wasn't watching. Rene thought it unhealthy for the other uncles to watch, especially Franko who wouldn't know what to do about sex even if he had the opportunity.

Rene looked up at the dormers. Doghouses. Or sheds. Not a fit place to take Ruthie, but then again she'd seen it plenty of times before.

In spite of his contrariness, when it got right down to it, Mack loved being Ruthie's fool. It was she led *him* into the house ... to John Ed's room, for suddenly the music came howling from John Ed's record player.

A light breeze stirred the hairball. It rolled toward Rene and stopped at her feet. She gave it a shove and sent it rolling again. Maybe men might make the world go round, but it was women kept it spinning.

Rene sighed and looked at Rut. She was inclined to scrape her whole self against a concrete wall, start over pink and new. She avoided the mirror, knowing how it ate time. No matter how close you drew the drapes, enough light was left for your reflection to startle you.

No need to primp for the grave. She could duck the mirror for weeks at a time, combing her hair and brushing her teeth by heart, but she had only to look at Rut to see the layers of time built up and hardened, and no way could the sloughing of the epidermis peel off the tough years.

You couldn't prick an old face with a pin. Hardening to shells, soon they'd be fossils. On top of it all, John Ed did not come home, nor call.

5

That evening the phone rang. Rene answered.

"This here Lilly Mabon," said a woman. "Your grandson down here with us. I want you to know he is safe."

"Otis's grandmother."

"Yes, that's right."

"Down at Mabon's Barbeque?"

"On Calhoun, yes."

"I'm much obliged. His grandpa and me will come fetch him."

"He could stay the night if he wants," said Lilly Mabon. "Morning would be soon enough. He come in real upset. Done calmed down some. Might be good if he rests hisself a little bit longer."

Rene heard a woman's wisdom in that voice.

"Miz Mabon, I don't want to put you out none."

"Be glad to have John Ed. I hear tell you been nice to my Otis. And we both know about raising grandsons. The two of them can do their lessons. Then they can play their music and eat some ribs. We all pitch in down here, so he'll have to help with the kitchen cleanup. It don't take long when everybody works together."

"Otis is real patient, puts up with John Ed's harp playing. I'm just saying it ain't easy. If he stays awhile, you might want to ball some cotton for your ears."

"John Ed wants to play harp real bad. One of these days he'll maybe surprise us all."

"Let's just hope it don't take too much longer."

***

The next morning they woke to snow-covered ground. Bird dog Rut insisted on going first to St. Patrick's to keep on schedule and give an estimate for the paint job.

"Don't do what you say you'll do and folks are liable to think you're unreliable. Afterwards we'll go down to Mabon's and pick up John Ed."

"Liable, unreliable, I like the sound of it. Might be a poem."

"Rene, you know well and good I know nothing about no poetry. You got a bad case of hearing what ain't there."

"I know what I hear, Rut Fury. What I'm hearing now is your stomach growling for lack of a fit breakfast."

"Franko and me ate toast. He's waiting in the truck. I want to get on the road before other folks start sliding around."

"I'm going, too," she said. "Just let me make up a lunch. The truck might stall out in the snow. We could get stranded."

"Make it small as you can, Rene, if that's possible. And make it quick."

"How fast I make it'll surprise you," she said, digging in the icebox. "Got half a ham in here. Can't keep a Fury stomach full without ham."

Rut looked at her.

"We ought to go on and just raise our own pigs. That way, if things get real bad and the sanitation workers up and quit like they talk about, the Fury pigs could gobble up the garbage and keep the whole neighborhood sanitary."

She reminded Rut that pig-stink was one of the world's great problems. "The pigs get harvested, but their smell don't go nowhere. It's how pigs get revenge."

"Forget the pig talk, Rene. Snow is coming down right proper now. Hurry it up, else I'm leaving without you."

"Yes, Sir Rut." Quickly she sliced ham, slathered mustard and mayo on the bread, wrapped the sandwiches in wax paper and stacked them in a grocery bag. "Rut, let me see if I have tater salad or chips."

"I'm leaving, Rene. Franko is out freezing in the truck and we don't need no side dishes."

Rene sighed and took up her coat from the hook by the back door. "OK, but when your stomach gets to growling, don't complain."

"When have I ever complained for lack of food, Rene?"

"There's always a first time, Rut Fury."

He went out the back door. Before she could slip on her galoshes, she heard the truck start up. She tucked the lunch bag under her arm, opened the door and stepped outside, nearly slipping on the back steps before climbing into the truck.

Rut eased down the driveway, the truck's exhaust billowing. She likened it to fog, imagining them in a boat on a river, sailing to some foreign port, Zanzibar or Africa. Where was Zanzibar anyhow? Maybe she'd look that up in the dictionary.

She climbed into the truck and got herself almost as comfortable as Franko, already snoring in the back seat in spite of the cold. What with the extra seat, the truck was a good investment, though she'd been opposed to the price of it.

Likely Franko would always be with them, whereas his brothers would no doubt leave home a second time to face the world on their own again.

At once the idea of having the population of the house thinned some was both exciting and fearful. All said, life seemed to be one stumble after another. Just as you get to feeling sure of yourself, you're bound to trip and fall flat on your face. No warning sign for heartbreak.

That was the thrill of it, the not knowing, being He went out the back door. Before she could slip on her galoshes, she heard the truck start up. She unawares then pow! If you was to live long enough you might even learn a little bit of everything there was to know, leastwise things near enough to bump into, secrets not in the Bible. She felt certain if time allowed, she'd come to know many things. She might even know Rut better than she knew herself.

Riding in the truck quieted her mind some. Down Southern Avenue they turned onto the Parkway, passing the Fairgrounds and Fairview Junior High, the trees already heavy with snow. They turned onto Union Avenue, passing big houses that people used to live in but were now mostly businesses.

They passed the beautiful Idlewild Presbyterian Church where the church people believe in predestination, something she well understood. Life is what it is.

Still and all, she thought about going there just to hear the preacher and the music, but knew she didn't own proper clothes. Maybe she'd save up and buy herself an outfit at the Helen Shop, a snooty store if truth be told. She doubted she'd ever darken the door. In the Helen Shop they'd think she was trying to raise above herself.

They crossed Belvedere and soon passed The House of Fine Paint where Rut knew everybody. If he got the bid today, he'd go there to buy paint for the church from Mr. Jim. She wondered how many gallons ... how ever did Rut figure all that out? A streak of genius, she figured, a talent way beyond her imagination. "How do you do it, Rut?"

"How do I do what, Rene?"

"How do you figure how much paint to buy?"

"Rene, it's no different than you figuring the groceries. How do you do it?

"I guess at it. Somehow it always comes out about right. Can't remember ever wasting one bite of food."

"Well, then both of us are smarter than most folks might think."

She felt a slight smile come onto her face and settled into her seat. Not hardly any traffic and so much to see: Berl Olswanger's Music Store where you could buy an instrument and take music lessons. "Rut, you think Mr. Olswanger could take on John Ed? Teach him to play?"

"You believe in miracles, Rene?"

She didn't bother to answer. They were paused, waiting for the traffic to pick up. At Crown Colony Shop a Chinese dragon looked to be hissing at the feet of a smiling pot-bellied Buddha. She wondered how the Chinese could pray to such a paunchy little god who grinned like a possum.

Across the street in the huge display window of Julius Lewis mannequin families were dressed-up for church: the women in short yellow and pink dresses, pill box hats with veils, and wrist length white gloves, the men and boys in light blue cord suits and cream colored hats circled with navy blue bands.

The little children were bow-tied and be-ribboned

in rainbow colors, carrying Easter baskets woven of straw. Giant eggs, rabbits and chickens dotted the bright green lawn behind a picket fence bordered in flowers.

"They call that a diorama," said Rut who knew just about everything and never bragged about it. For Rene the display promised redemption, though Old Man Winter might just up and spoil it all.

"Rut, when we get back home, I could make some Easter eggs and you could paint us a big picture with rabbits and flowers, and maybe some butterflies. Give us all some Easter spirit."

"Tired of my mules, are you?"

"Don't get you feelings hurt. I'm real fond of some of them mules."

Still and all, how was it that Rut kept on painting mules, one after the other over and again, and never get wore out with a one of them.

Could be love, she thought, smiling inside herself. Painting mules was what Rut looked forward to, what kept him going.

Still, there didn't seem to be any surprises left for him to put down on his canvas. Teeth maybe, though he'd already painted real strange sets of teeth--snaggle teeth, buckteeth, no teeth at all.

Then the ears: lop-ears, bristling ears and ears akimbo. The mules expressions told the real story--

stubborn was what, as stubborn as the man who painted them.

She looked at him now, his teeth protruding a little, his ears poked from his cap, big ears that curled on the tips, and suddenly it came into her head that every mule he painted was his own self portrait.

6

"He's right handsome," she observed, passing the deviled eggs while admiring the statue of Nathan Bedford Forrest. "His horse, too. About as handsome as a horse gets." She popped an egg into her mouth. "Forrest Park," she said as if the name of the park had just occurred to her.

Rut said, "Some folks didn't like the general, said he was bad. Others said he was smart, nigh on to a genius. Likely he was a little bit of both, the way it is with most folks. A little good, a little bad."

Franko took two eggs, swallowed them both whole and went back to his napping. Rut ate one slowly and declined another.

Rene then turned her attention back to the row of buildings they'd just passed. "The Medical School could use some sprucing up," she declared. "Schools what teach how to cure folks ought to look neat and clean."

She ate the last egg. Somebody had to.

"That building back there is old as Methuselah," said Rut. "Not much you could do to fix it up. It just is what it is."

Above the arched doorway a mysterious carved face wearing a hood seemed in a brood. As the students passed under it, Rene though they probably dreaded being cooped up in there on a fine snowy day. She said, "I heard students practice on the dead."

"I painted in there a time or two," said Rut. "Never felt comfortable. I'd get to worrying about the cadavers. If I'd known any of 'um before."

They passed Sun Studio where Rene knew the best musicians made their records. Elvis, mostly. "Johnny Cash played in there, didn't he?" she asked, knowing full well the answer. "Sam Phillips was in charge."

Franko was still looking back at the carved face, his head craning. "Maybe those students are going in there to operate on a dead man right now. Maybe they're going to take out his tonsils. Maybe they're going to take out his eyes or cut off his ears."

Rene patted his knee and shook her head, trying not to think of the dead bodies.

"Long before the school was built, Chickasaw Indians lived around here." She was just thinking up something to say so Franko wouldn't think too much about the dead. "Maybe the Indians lived right about here," she said, pointing. She imagined the snow-covered cars at the dealership as a village of Chickasaw huts and herself as a pioneer woman riding in a wagon, hoping the ox pulling the wagon wouldn't up and die down before reaching their destination.

Likely a lot of the pioneers settled wherever they stopped, just went along with natural disaster and didn't try to fight it.

That was how life was—build a shelter and do your best to make it a fit place to spend your days--hoeing, tilling the ground, planting vegetables. You took in the manners you saw and heard from the folks you met and adjusted yourself accordingly.

And suddenly Rut parked the truck, St. Patrick's Church looming above them.

"Rene, remember to quiet down when we get in the church proper."

"Rut Fury, it's been a while since I been in church, but I know how to act in the Lord's house. Only thing is I wish John Ed was here with us. I guess he's having a nice rest down there with the Negroes."

"We'll pick him up shortly. John Ed ain't their responsibility."

"Sure is nice to have a rest from his music."

"Can't deny it. The ringing in my ears has cleared

up some. Lately, I'd thought I might be going deaf."

"Why not pick him up now? Let him see the big church. Might be a good thing for him altogether."

"You got a scheme going, Rene? I wouldn't put it past you?"

"I don't know what you mean, Rut Fury."

Then Rene paused as if a scheme had just occurred to her. She hummed a little tune and wondered where it had come from. Had she learned it or had she made it up? She'd kind of missed John Ed's awful music.

They trudged up the steps and into St. Patrick's.

Father John met them in the vestibule and led them into the church proper. Above the hand of God reached for the angels and saints. She figured he was pulling them into Heaven and wondered what it might be like up there beyond the clouds. Would there be anything to eat? If she ended up in heaven, would she be cooking for Saints?

She steered Franko into a pew. They sat while Rut and Father John walked around the church. She felt peaceful yet small under the dome.

Mostly, she wondered what the day might bring and if they'd get John Ed back and if he'd come on home where he belonged and would he see it that way. She doubted he'd come back willingly.

7

The sky was boiling in crows, the beating of wings loud and fearful. "Some say crows are shadows of the dead," said Rut.

Near the train station on Calhoun, the moodiness of the cloudy sky and the cawing crows followed Rene, Rut and Franko into Bobo's Barbecue like something you'd drag on a string.

Vidella Mabon—a izable woman in a pink hair net—stood in the middle of the kitchen at the chopping block, whacking onions with her cleaver.

"Ought not allow folks to come back here in the kitchen expecting a special supper. We got to start in cooking lunch at sunup, and then we got to serve and clean up. We catches a couple of fitful z's on old cots ain't worth keeping, dreaming about pigs the whole time...pigs snorting and running after you--they'll do that, you know--get you down on the ground and eat you alive, and you wake up hollering and swallowing your own tongue. Then we starts in on supper. Day, night, No-luck folks coming and going. Lord have mercy."

Uncle Timbs glared at her.

"If no-luck folks didn't have pig, they wouldn't have no luck at all. Vidella, serve these folks a real nice meal and let them eat it in peace."

"They'll git what I got when I git it! Fire is just

like a man," she said while turning to the Bobos. "Don't want to start in the morning. Don't want to quit at night."

"Excuse me, ma'am," said Rut. "We're John Ed's grandparents. And this here is John Ed's Uncle Franko. Mighty obliged you took John Ed in last night. Seems like you got enough on your plate. We come to fetch him."

"I figured out who ya'll were. We were glad to have John Ed. I'm Otis' Aunt Vidella. Ya'll can call me Vidella."

She pointed them to a table and to the menu on the wall above the kitchen lookout. John Ed and Otis came in, a sheepish John Ed nodding toward his grandparents and uncle.

Vidella said, "Now sit yourself down and get comfortable."

Little Walter's tremolo played on the jukebox. Otis played along, John Ed watching silently.

Vidella brought Rut and Rene plates of barbecue, slaw and beans.

"Otis, play us some church music, something pretty."

Instead Otis started in playing Little Walter's *Juke* just as five or six burly black men wearing worn-out coats, scruffy shoes and battered hats came into the room carrying signs. The men, noisy and hungry, propped the signs near the front door: JUSTICE.....BOYCOTT......AFSCME.....DO RIGHT, MR MAYOR, for months now the men threatening a garbage strike.

Uncle Timbs said, "Slack time coming to an end."

Chloe waits on the men. "Same as always, right?"

Uncle Timbs came to Rut and Rene's table.

"Don't pay any mind to what's said. These are some hard times. Mayor Mule says the men can't have no union, but Mayor Mule ain't God."

"That's right," said a man at the next table.

Other men answered him in kind. "You know it, Brother...Go on. Go on."

Vidella spieled off the dessert specials—banana pudding, lemon chiffon pie, black bottom pie. The men were salivating. "Mercy, mercy."

"Don't give me none of that. You sitting around here worrying over dessert and how to pay for it while the Government of the U.S. of A. planning to send a white men to the moon! Only way a black man going to the moon if they need somebody to pick up the trash."

"Sure is so."

"Ain't it the truth."

Clattering dishes, Chloe cleared a booth. "Get even is what I say. You got more reason than most."

"You got to be even before you its even," said Vidella. "We all got some catching up to do."

"That's right," said Rene, thinking aloud — "the catching up to do."

"Uncle Timbs looked up at the ceiling light, the answers alive in its glow. "Our time is coming. It ain't going to be if and when no more ... it's going to be now or never! When the garbage starts smelling real bad, white folks going to pay us some mind."

Rene felt herself witnessing something never before seen, her head heavy with the weight of it. Soon after, things got rough in Memphis. Army tanks rolled on home ground and she'd wonder what would come next.

Hundreds of signs: I AM A MAN — that's when it got real.

THE END

Cold Eye

Cold Eye

67064237R00130

Made in the USA
Charleston, SC
03 February 2017